CAPTIVE

A key turned. The cabin door banged open and the pirate captain strode in.

"I am the master of this ship and your benefactor, Jules LeFevre. Let us understand each other from the very beginning. "You"—he pointed at Sister Augustine—"will not be harmed unless you become a troublemaker."

Relieved that Sister Augustine's life would be spared, Reyna could not keep from wondering, *What of me?* She dared not move to bring the captain's wrath upon her. His personality was so strong she felt smothered.

Suddenly, Jules LeFevre rose from his chair, grabbed Reyna's hand, and rotated her in a circle, then pulled her close against him.

"And you, my pet. I have special plans for you."

Reyna's Reward

WANDA DIONNE

AN AVON FLARE BOOK

REYNA'S REWARD is an original publication of Avon Books. This work has never before appeared in book form.

AVON BOOKS
A division of
The Hearst Corporation
1350 Avenue of the Americas
New York, New York 10019

Copyright © 1996 by Wanda Dionne
Excerpt from *Sofia's Heart* copyright © 1996 by Sharon Cadwallader
Published by arrangement with the author
Library of Congress Catalog Card Number: 96-96184
ISBN: 0-380-78476-9
RL: 6.1

First Avon Flare Printing: October 1996

AVON FLARE TRADEMARK REG. U.S. PAT. OFF. AND IN OTHER COUNTRIES, MARCA REGISTRADA, HECHO EN U.S.A.

Printed in the U.S.A.

RA   10 9 8 7 6 5 4 3 2 1

To my father,
Capt. Lynn O. Hodges,
for instilling in me
a sense of adventure
and a love for the sea

And to my mother,
Cassie Tuma Hodges,
for teaching me to love history
and cherish tradition

Acknowledgments

Special thanks to Wanda Lee Dickey of New Orleans, Louisiana, a Jean Lafitte enthusiast; and Lisa May, archivist, Diocese of Galveston-Houston, Texas.

Chapter 1

Spring, 1814
The Gulf of Mexico

Reyna Maria Alvaron cowered in the darkest corner of the ship's cabin, cringing every time she heard a new scream of pain or a blood-curdling yell. Even with her hands covering her ears, she could hear the muffled sounds of battle overhead.

The sharp clang of metal upon metal rang out as saber met cutlass. She heard crashes, bumps and thumps, the splash of objects being thrown overboard. The ship shuddered at every cannon blast. Smoke singed the air.

Sister Augustine bravely faced the bolted door, a heavy flintlock pistol clutched in her shaking hands. The Spanish captain had loaded it before he left to join the battle. One lead ball stood between them and unknown agony, and it was anybody's guess whether the good Sister could pull the trigger anyway.

The pirate ship stalked them through the morning fog, the captain said, coming up out of the burned-off mist too fast and too close to outrun. Cutthroats were now on board, and Reyna wondered how the Spanish crew would fare against them.

"They're coming, *querida*," whispered Sister Augustine. The feisty nun planted her feet in a firm stance and braced her shoulders against the wooden pillar that supported the ceiling of their simple quarters. They had shared this cabin almost twenty-four hours a day for five weeks during the slow, often storm-tossed voyage from Spain.

The door handle rattled. Curses rang out. A heavy object crashed against the portal, time and time again, until the wood splintered and the pirates broke through. The room seemed to vibrate. Reyna crouched farther back in her hiding place and peeked around the corner.

A deeply tanned pirate, with an unkempt beard and a bandanna covering his head, burst into the tiny room. Several ruffians stood guard at the entryway. They leered at the frightened nun as the gun wavered in her hands.

"Ah! Holy One!" the swarthy sailor said. "What are you doing with a weapon? Surely, you would betray your sacred vows if you were to shoot me, Picou, dead." His sinister laughter chilled Reyna as thoroughly as had the icy wind sweeping across the Atlantic.

"Why are you aboard this puny vessel?" The evil-looking pirate jerked the gun out of Sister's grasp.

Defenseless and outraged, she stood her ground. "Do not advance one step further, young man. Even you could not stand against God's wrath if you were to harm me." Her voice wavered, but she held her head high so that she could look down her nose at the blustering pirate.

"Holy Mary, Mother of God, I would not harm

2

nary a hair on your head—if hair be growing there. Come now. Let us leave this airless pit. Come topside and meet my captain.''

The good Sister signaled from behind her skirts for Reyna to remain hidden. The grizzled sailor escorted the nun out of the cabin, but the girl fully expected the raiders to turn around and come back for her.

Fresh air slowly filtered into the tiny cabin from the open door, and Reyna began to breathe again. She was sure she had held her breath for the last ten minutes. Compared to moments before, the ship now seemed to be sitting still on an ocean of glass.

A deafening silence replaced the battle noise.

She waited what seemed an eternity, lulled by the splish-splash of water against the wooden hull and the cry of a lone gull riding the wind. Surely she had not been abandoned. Surely Sister Augustine would not leave her here to die . . . unless death was a better fate than what lay ahead with the pirates . . . or, Heaven forbid, the good Sister had already met her own end at the hands of those wicked men.

Reyna slowly crept to the door, listened, then padded on bare feet to the ship's ladder that led topside. Once she climbed the steep steps, she would be immediately exposed, but Reyna had lost all patience for cringing below in fear. *It is better by far to face what lies ahead, than to skulk in the shadows.*

Reyna started up the ladder. She glimpsed above her the ripple of white sails against a blue-gray sky. Suddenly it seemed critical that she gain the deck and be free of her confinement.

When her head cleared the hold, she was revived by a deep breath of clean salt air. But then a man's steely voice, with the hint of a French accent, startled her from behind.

"Ah, my little beauty," he said pleasantly. "We've been wondering when you would appear."

Chapter 2

A man of indeterminate age stepped forward, reaching out a hand to help her gain the deck. His skin was weathered by sun and salt air. Long black hair flowed past his shoulders. Dark eyebrows hooded heartless gray eyes.

Reyna assumed he was the captain of the pirate ship, but she couldn't give him much attention for her eyes were drawn to Sister Augustine. The nun's arms were pinned behind her back by a mountainous man with a shaved head.

Muscles rippled across his bare chest. He held Sister with one hand and covered her mouth with the other, preventing her from crying out a warning.

"Here, m'lady, sit yourself upon this bloody crate." The pirate captain kicked a wooden box toward Reyna.

She shrank into herself, her dark gaze darting from person to person in an effort to assess the danger.

"Loose the Sister, Tomas," directed the pirate. The sailor giant immediately set her free.

The cutthroat captain addressed his crew. "I've heard about the passage of young Spanish beauties to men of substance in the Americas. If I did such a deed, I would be hung from the highest yardarm—but not these holy women who prey upon children.''

His brooding eyes remained riveted on Reyna. ''Tell me, Sister, does your orphanage rescue only the ragtags who show promise of intelligence and beauty?''

Silent, Sister Augustine edged toward the girl.

Reyna assumed all the dignity the Catholic sisters had insisted on during her ten years at Our Mother of Mercy convent and orphanage. Resolutely, she stepped toward Sister Augustine. She grasped the older woman's hands and pressed them against her bosom to still her own runaway heart. Her back was turned to the pirate captain.

''Where are you bound, my beautiful one?'' The captain circled the two women. One hand smoothed his moustache while the other rested threateningly on the hilt of his sword. ''Ah! You probably aren't allowed to speak to strangers. A man like me is below your station. Correct?''

Sister Augustine pulled Reyna into a suffocating embrace and whispered, ''You are safe for the moment, my child. You are worth more in gold to them if you remain untouched, unblemished. Do not vex them.''

''What about you?'' asked Reyna.

''I am safe, too, for they still hold some respect for the Mother Church.''

A hateful voice interrupted their hushed conversation.

''Come, senorita, let me look at you. It is I to whom you should be whispering. Come, stand before me. Let me see my prize.''

He spun Reyna away from the nun. ''Could this female child be worth a large ransom? She seems dull-witted, although I see the possibility of beauty yet to bloom.''

Reyna's face flushed as though she'd been slapped. *Heed the nun's warning—do not vex him.* She was confused, vulnerable. Her brain flashed warning signals, but her heart convinced her he would not harm her.

Reyna had never been this close to a man before, except for the priests. She hugged herself, perplexed, needing to say something, but what? ''Sir,'' she said, ''we have not been introduced.''

The captain shook his head in mock disgust, but a glint of interest lingered in his gray eyes. ''What have the nuns done to you, my pet? Have they crushed your very spirit? Have they destroyed every ounce of fiery Spanish sentiment that runs in your veins?'' He rubbed his calloused thumb across her cheekbone.

Reyna recoiled.

''I am your master,'' he said, spacing out each word for emphasis. ''That is all you need to know. Now tell me, who are you?'' His manner seemed to run both hot and cold.

''I am Reyna Maria Alvaron. I am sixteen years old, and I'm on my way to marry a very important man.'' She tilted her head upward so she could meet his strange eyes, then abruptly looked down, chilled with fright. ''His name is Don Carlos Xavier Vasquez, and he expects us to arrive in New Orleans within the week.''

Reyna swallowed her fear. ''Sir,'' she continued, ''we are just one weary Holy Sister and me. Do not harm us. Please.''

''Ma cherie.'' He caressed her long raven hair, then, with a sharp twist, brought it tight behind her

head. He pulled her away from the nun and up close against him.

Reyna strained to get away but his grasp tightened. Sister slipped to her knees in the posture of prayer, begging for mercy from God, from the pirate, from whoever would listen.

"Gather their belongings, Picou." The captain spoke to the sailor who had seized Sister Augustine from their cabin. "They will come with us," he said. "Take them to my quarters while I decide their fate."

Suddenly he thrust Reyna away from him. "You bore me, child! You act as if all the joy of living has been sucked from your soul."

Picou's eyebrows raised in a crazy leer. "The girl has probably never experienced the joy of living. 'Tis a shame." He laughed at his own joke. "Come along, ladies." He ushered them to the gangplank and half-pushed, half-carried them across to the larger vessel tied alongside. Tomas lumbered along behind.

They descended an elegantly carved wooden staircase, where Picou showed them into a large opulent cabin, then locked them in. Tomas rumbled a reply to Picou's order. Apparently, the big man would guard them. From what, they did not know.

"What will happen to us?" whispered Reyna.

"I can't say, my dear. We must pray for God's protection." Sister dropped to her knees.

Reyna, wearing a homespun gown, hesitated long enough to note the gold dinnerware on the table, Italian tile and marble, plush skins covering the ornate brass single bed. As she bowed her knees in the familiar pattern of prayer, Reyna stared at the wealth displayed around her and wondered if her life had taken a turn for better or worse.

Chapter 3

Tejas, Texas

"We're ready, Don Carlos." Benito Cruz Sandoval expertly reined his horse in front of Don Carlos Xavier Vasquez, who beckoned him over to the supply wagon he was inspecting.

Don Carlos issued last minute orders to the driver before he turned toward Benito. The younger man dismounted and they shook hands.

With an uplifted hand, Don Carlos warded off any comments. "You're the only man I trust to do this errand, Benito. Ship the nun back to Spain and give her these gold coins as an extra token. Then bring my Reyna to me—pure and beautiful as I know she will be."

"Are you sure this arrangement is to your advantage?" Benito asked once again. "I mean, buying a bride, sight unseen. A young girl, too. She might not be fit for breeding. She might be sickly. . . . She might look down her aristocratic European nose at us."

Don Carlos knew very little about his bride except her name, age, and confirmed innocence.

"Benito, *compadre,* my friend, we've been over this a hundred times. The women I have known were tainted. Worldly. Not fit to mother my children. I'm in my thirties. If I'm ever going to have a family, I must do it now. Bring her safely back to me, Benito."

The young man snapped a half-hearted salute. *El Capitan,* the former master of a sailing ship, was now crippled, land-bound and dry-docked, but he still commanded Benito's respect and quick obedience.

Benito's mind wandered to the many evenings he and his former shipmaster had slouched on the cowhide sofas in front of the stone fireplace of the adobe ranch house. These comradely evenings surely would end when Don Carlos took a wife.

Was he jealous? Yes, he was.

"Move out." Benito waved the vaqueros onward. They would leave the carriage and half the supplies at Snake Island, sail to New Orleans, collect the girl and return by the same route. When her carriage left El Camino Real, the young woman would, in effect, bid farewell to civilization.

Benito slumped as he trotted toward the distant gate, hoping the set of his shoulders informed Don Carlos of his displeasure.

Chapter 4

Aboard ship

A key turned. The cabin door banged open and the pirate captain strode in, disturbing the women at prayer. Reyna's knees were stiff, so it was difficult for her to rise quickly enough to please him. Roughly, he hauled her to a standing position.

"Ladies," he announced, "it is time we got to know each other better." He collapsed into the chair at the head of the elaborately set dinner table.

"What shall we call you, sir?" asked Sister Augustine, calmly rising to her full height of less than five feet.

"Yes, yes, you are still determined that we abide by all the conventions, aren't you, woman? First, let me introduce my mate, Picou, a seaman from the old school. He can sail through the wildest gales and remain on course. He is fearless and resourceful. To Picou and Tomas, I have given your charge. They will guard you with their lives, if need be."

Picou grinned and swept his bandanna off, aiming a bow toward the two women.

"I digress; forgive me," said the captain. "I am the master of this ship and your benefactor, Jules LeFevre. My ship and my crew operate under the authority of Jean Lafitte out of Barataria. You have heard of him?"

He did not wait for an answer. "Let us understand each other from the very beginning. You,"—he pointed at Sister Augustine—"will not be harmed in any way, *unless* you become a troublemaker. You will not, however, return to Spain and this convent that sells children. Our own little community in the bayous has need of a religious. You will do nicely."

"But what about Friar Tuck?" Picou asked.

"Yes, yes, Father Francis, our priest who robs from the rich and gives to the poor, an educated man of God straight out of the tales of *Robin Hood.* You will be a help to him, I am sure, but, more important, it is our women who need a mother comforter. Ships return home without sailors, children die from the fever, a baby is stillborn. Our grieving women are overcome with soul-searching questions. Dear Sister, you will put their minds to rest."

Relieved that Sister Augustine's life would be spared, Reyna could not keep from wondering, *What of me? What of me?* The cry resounded inside her head and her heart, but she dared not make a sudden move to bring the captain's wrath upon her. His personality was so strong, she felt smothered when he was near.

Suddenly, Jules LeFevre rose from his chair, grabbed Reyna's hand, and rotated her in a circle as though they were dancing. He whirled her around three or four times, then pulled her close against him.

"As for you, my pet. I have special plans."

Reyna trembled and, under his intense scrutiny, lowered her eyes.

"Look at me, girl! Have you no fight in you? Speak."

She did not reply.

"I'm taking you to Barataria as my prize. Your Don Carlos will die of old age waiting for you, or he will pay a devil's ransom to get you back. Lafitte will decide."

Reyna glanced toward Sister Augustine, seeking permission to speak. The nun nodded, but before she could say anything, Jules ordered Picou to move the Sister to another cabin.

The man's brusque "Come" was softened by a sheepish smile. "You will be safe with me."

"Reyna?" Sister Augustine reached for the girl's hand.

"No, not yet, your ward remains here—with me. I wish to have more knowledge of her."

Chapter 5

"So." Jules removed his sword and scabbard, and loosened his shirt at the neck, revealing curling black hairs on his broad, tanned chest. He poured water into a blue ceramic bowl and splashed it on his face.

Reyna wondered if this was symbolic of washing the blood away after battle, or maybe in preparation for sacrifice . . . her own?

"Girl?" Jules flung himself backward onto the bed, arms wide, legs spread. Then he shifted to lean on one elbow. "You are a meek little mouse next to the fiery women who inhabit my world."

Reyna was terrified.

"It is as though you are a willow in a windstorm— blowing this way and that, bending to the will of anyone stronger. Why are you like this?" His brow furrowed into a worry line, but his voice was softer and gentler than before.

Reyna drew a deep breath into her lungs. She stammered, "I have never been near a man before, except the kindly priest who came for Mass and confession."

"And . . . ?"

"And I am afraid of you." She squared her shoulders and stared back at him. Their eyes locked.

"What of this rich man you have promised to wed?"

"It was all arranged by the good sisters."

When Reyna was six years old, her parents died in a fire that almost wiped out their small village in the Spanish interior. She had no other relatives, and the people who lived in the village were poor. No one wanted another mouth to feed. The local priest hitched her a ride on a hay wagon to San Leandro's orphanage, run by the good sisters. Constant prayer and tedious drudgery became her life.

This was her first venture away from the convent. The sisters said it was her chance to break away from the mold, to create a home for a wealthy husband, to bring grace, beauty and salvation to a heathen world.

Jules bent toward her and took her hands into his. "I see your potential for beauty—but no man wants a mere doll to play with. He wants a woman with light in her eyes and fire in her heart. Even your dull Spanish lord will desire more from you than beauty and breeding."

Reyna tried to pull out of his grasp. "I don't know what you want," she cried in desperation.

"I can understand your fear of me, but even in the most remote convent, surely you have heard enough rumors to know what will be expected of you when you wed. Don't pretend to be so naive. Wake up! Show me some spunk!"

Abruptly he took her in his arms, and swayed with

her to the rocking of the ship. Reyna froze, making no move to return his ardor or to escape.

Jules gripped her shoulders with a bruising pressure. "And now, my love, I shall explain your position on this ship. You belong to me!"

Chapter 6

A few minutes later, Tomas led Reyna to the cabin where Sister waited.

"What does he want from me?" Reyna cried, as she fell into the lower bunk.

"I don't know, child, but we must continue to ask for God's protection. Surely it is not His will for us to die at the hands of these barbarians. But if it is, then we must do so with dignity."

Reyna rolled onto her stomach. She closed her eyes, silently begging for salvation; but her prayers were soon forgotten as the rocking waters lulled her to sleep.

Both women were startled when Picou unlocked the door and swaggered in, unbidden. A gold tooth glinted when he grinned at them.

"The capt'n sent this dress and these jewels, m'lady. Wear 'em like a queen." He chuckled. "We dine royally tonight to celebrate our conquests. Dinner is at eight. I'll come for you." Picou winked, then left the room.

Sister Augustine sagged onto a bench. "My child . . . I have the impression this is a special occasion tonight and you are the guest of honor."

The crimson velvet gown, trimmed with gold braid, was the height of extravagance. But on diminutive Reyna, it had the effect of a child playing dress-up in her mother's clothes.

Sister Augustine rummaged through the basket of sewing utensils Picou had brought in and began making alterations. Sister had mended clothes at the convent, but never a gown like this one. She smiled, then, aloud, asked forgiveness for the sin of self-indulgence. After placing a gold necklace around Reyna's neck, Sister clipped a large emerald brooch to both the necklace and the gown to pull the bodice high enough so that Reyna's chest would not be exposed. Then she piled the girl's dark hair high on her head and anchored it with a jeweled comb.

The only thing lacking was shoes. Reyna's slippers had been left on board the Spanish ship.

A key clanged in the metal opening and the wooden door scraped against the floor as it was thrown open. "Are you ready, ladies?" Picou was silent as he took in Reyna's coiffed hair, the enormous brooch, the velvet gown, and her bare feet. "Jolly good! The captain will be delighted."

With all the dignity she could summon, Reyna marched royally into the stateroom to be greeted by the admiring stares of Captain Jules LeFevre and two of his officers.

"You look ravishing, my dear. And, Holy Sister, it appears you have a talent that can be put to good use when we reach land. I compliment you, a very creative approach."

With a lift of her eyebrow and a jerk of her head, the nun reminded Reyna to observe the formalities. Reyna curtsied and advanced to the place the captain indicated next to him.

"You seem to have found some cheer in the last few hours, my lady. It becomes you." His eyes traveled from her flushed face to her bare toes and he guffawed. "Ah! Now I see the reason for your good humor. A joke. On me?"

"I'm sorry, Captain. The gown and the jewels, with certain adjustments, could be made to fit, but nowhere did we find any shoes," Sister said.

Dinner was an elaborate affair but the men ate like pigs, the so-called officers tearing at their food as if they were marauding, starving animals. Repulsed by their lack of manners, Reyna was made even more uncomfortable by the glazed stare of Jules LeFevre.

After dinner, he shoved away from the table, lounged back with one leg over the arm of his chair, and lit a cheroot. One nod toward the door, and his officers abruptly departed.

The girl licked her lips from nervousness. "Don Carlos Vasquez will be waiting in New Orleans," she said. "You do intend to allow Sister Augustine and me to continue our journey, don't you?"

Jules slapped his thigh and laughed. "Lafitte will decide your fate, not I. But don't get any false hopes. He is a rare businessman. He would only let you go if it meant more money for his pockets. You are no longer a person, my dear. You are a commodity."

Reyna swallowed and tried again. "If I stay at Barataria, what role will I play?"

"Ah, there you go again. What role, you ask? Why, be yourself, my dear."

"Perhaps," she said, with a faltering smile, "perhaps I will have to get to know myself first."

"Yes, this may be so," he agreed. "But I intend to help you make many discoveries."

∽∽∽

Chapter 7

New Orleans

Benito Cruz Sandoval was stumped. He had haunted the New Orleans wharves for most of a week, but the Spanish vessel had yet to appear. Plenty of flatboats loaded and unloaded for runs up the Mississippi River. Merchant ships from exotic ports of call filled their holds with sugar and molasses, rice, lumber, beef, and tobacco.

The levee bustled with activity. Slaves from Africa and the West Indies rolled huge cotton bales along the wharves, and ebony-skinned women balanced baskets of bread on their shoulders. American Indians and farmers from outlying districts sold their wares at the public market near the levee. Businessmen took refreshment at the popular New Orleans coffee houses, their voices raised in discussion of America's current war with England, and the Napoleonic wars in Europe.

Brawls were common, but that didn't concern Benito. He could handle himself in any fight. He was worried, though, because there had been no word on the long overdue Spanish ship. It was as if she had vanished with no trace.

Benito's vaqueros took to the bawdy New Orleans streets with gusto. They said they were tired of waiting for a ship that most likely was resting on the bottom of the sea. Benito refused to believe the worst because he couldn't bear returning to the Anchorage in Tejas without Don Carlos's precious Reyna. Benito decided to give it another week.

Benito Cruz Sandoval was ten years younger than the man he served. They met when Benito, then a fourteen-year-old ragtag from a Mexican coastal shantytown, appeared at the gangplank of Don Carlos's ship with the *policia* in hot pursuit. The captain hid the boy under a barrel, sent the authorities packing, then offered Benito a berth on his vessel as a general lackey. The sea was a wonderful escape, Benito thought, and he thanked God for sending him to the *Madeira Maiden*.

At the age of twenty-four, Don Carlos had been a cocky yet seasoned sailing master. *El Capitan* became a god to Benito. He gave Benito a home, taught him to navigate and chart, to read the stars and the colors of the ocean.

There'd been lessons in manhood, too. Under Carlos's tutelage, Benito fleshed out and matured. He climbed the riggings, loaded cargo, visited bars, even drew his weapon in several "to the death" duels.

Then their ship had floundered on the coral reef off Cuba. Cutthroats moved in for the kill. Carlos refused to give up his ship and, instead, directed Benito to set it afire. Don Carlos's intention was to go down in flames along with his precious cargo. But

21

then his knee was smashed by a lead ball, and he fell unconscious to the deck.

Benito loaded him into a dinghy and paddled like a crazy man toward the shore beyond the reef. Finally, they cleared a jutting rock and were sheltered. The boy wedged the boat among boulders, covered Carlos with a canvas sail, and went to find help in a nearby village.

El Capitan's recovery was slow—as much mental as it was physical. Benito was credited with saving Carlos's life, but there was little he could do to help the man overcome the effect of all his losses.

Eventually Carlos wrote to his father, admitting misfortune and defeat. The Spanish merchant sent a personal messenger with a line of credit, a title, plenty of cash, and a Spanish land grant for vast acreage in the South Tejas wilderness.

With Benito's help, Don Carlos rebuilt his life. Now he wanted a wife, and he had sent Benito to get her. Benito refused to return without the girl. *El Capitan* was counting on him, and Benito would not let him down.

Now the young mestizo swiped at the dust on his flannel pants, and replaced his leather hat on the back of his head. Benito had seen so much sun and sea at an early age that a fine network of crinkles were already etched at the corners of his eyes, making him look older than his twenty years. He was taller than most Mexican youths, slender with a wiry build.

Where was that Spanish ship anyway? How much longer should I wait? How can I face El Capitan without the girl? Another week had passed with no word, and Benito had dismissed his vaqueros that morning, sending them back to inform Don Carlos of the delay. They carried with them his sealed personal letter, wax imprinted with the ring Don Carlos had given him. It had been a hard letter to write. He told of his intentions to wait a while longer for the Spanish ship, but he admitted his concerns and apologized in advance should he not be able to satisfactorily complete his mission.

Seated at an outdoor cafe, he was reflecting on his predicament when someone called his name.

"Hey, Sandoval, come see what I got." The trader, who had befriended him, interrupted his daydream.

Benito swallowed the last of his coffee and followed the merchant to a stack of boxes and crates.

"Looks like tapestry. What's so special?"

"This particular piece comes from the Leandro region in Spain. Isn't that where your orphan was bound from?"

Benito's interest quickened. "Where did you get this?"

"I hate to tell you, but this was part of a shipment that came in last night from Barataria."

"Pirates?"

"Yep! But they call themselves privateers. If your gal was captured by them rascals, I doubt she'll be of any good use now." The man hesitated. "I did hear one of their ships came in heavy laden the other day. The ship mastered by LeFevre. He's a particularly cussed varmint."

Pirates again, Benito thought. *They took Don Carlos's ship, smashed his leg beyond repair, and now they've stolen his woman.*

Chapter 8

Aboard ship

Reyna placed her largest valise outside the cabin, just as she had been ordered, leaving the door open a crack so she could question whoever came for their belongings. Their trunks had appeared in the passageway outside their room during the night. A shiver of excitement wormed its way under her skin and she felt a little breathless.

She had taken special care in dressing this morning, wearing the gown Sister picked out for her—the one she'd been saving for her first meeting with the man she was going to marry. It seemed more important now to impress Jean Lafitte, for he was the new master of her fate. He would decide the course of her life.

Tomas startled Reyna when he suddenly appeared at the door. How could such a big man move so silently? He jerked his head toward the stairway, but Sister Augustine held Reyna back so that she could go first.

The set of the woman's chin and the glint in her

dark eyes warned Reyna that Sister was on a rampage. After last night's dinner and the late deckside stroll with Captain LeFevre, Sister said she was more convinced than ever that Reyna was in danger of losing her innocence. The girl denied she felt any attraction at all for the suave pirate, but Sister Augustine said she could read the signs. Today she would demand their release.

Topside, her head bobbing and finger pointing accusingly, Sister Augustine spoke privately with Jules. Whatever he said, the nun reeled backward as if she'd been slapped. Her face paled, and her hands nervously sought her Rosary.

Reyna clutched her small tote against her chest, and wandered to the ship's railing to look over the side. She didn't want to be part of any new confrontation. She'd had enough excitement yesterday.

It was noon on a warm April day, with the sun already bearing down upon them. Reyna fleetingly wondered what summer would be like in this new land.

She knew she looked her best, and immediately confessed the sin of pride. Her gown was a rosebud print set against a soft, creamy background. Crochet scalloped the modest neckline, and the front of the dress was layered with ruffles that peeked from beneath a poufed overskirt. She was wearing her black lace-up shoes that Captain LeFevre had actually sent someone to retrieve from the Spanish ship before it was scuttled.

"Ah, m'lady. What do we have here?" Jules strode toward her, an ashen-faced Sister Augustine following timorously behind. He ripped the small bag out of Reyna's grip. "Would you be taking my jewels with you? They were gifts for the evening, not for eternity." The look from his gray eyes was penetrating, but a smirk dawdled under his moustache, as if he were secretly delighted to accuse her of thievery.

Reyna's hand flew to her mouth in shock. "The jewels are in our cabin, sir, with the velvet dress—on the dressing table. I knew they did not belong to me."

"God rest the souls to whom they did belong," Sister Augustine intoned, as she tried, half-heartedly, to insinuate herself between Reyna and the captain.

Jules jerked his head toward Tomas, and the big man shambled away in the direction of the ship's ladder. It was obvious Tomas already had his orders.

Sister whispered to Reyna, "He said he'd just as soon kill me as listen to my complaints." Sister gulped. "I believe him."

Reyna felt herself recoil with shock. *Could this be true? Are our lives worth so little?*

Silently, the three of them watched the activity below until Tomas returned, the emerald brooch resting in his hand.

Jules pinned it to the bodice of Reyna's gown, his fingers lingering slightly longer than necessary. "Now this jewel belongs to you, my dear. Guard it well."

Reyna curtsied.

"On with you now," Jules said. "Tomas will take you ashore by an indirect route. It is safer for you. Picou and I must remain here. We have much to do."

Reyna swallowed her anger as she studied the small craft bobbing at the waterline, but Sister Augustine complained again. "The boats do not look safe. They are too small, too skimpy. Having come this far, now do you wish us to drown?"

"Quiet, woman! Your safety is at risk—but not from these boats or boatmen. Tomas will sneak you ashore, to Lafitte. You will be placed in his caretaking. Otherwise, there are those among us who would eat you alive—the same as the alligators in the bayous. And if you don't shush your incessant complaining, I might do the job myself!"

Tomas made a surefooted descent on the rope ladder and stepped onto a large raft. When it steadied, he motioned for Reyna to join him.

She hesitated, but Jules scooped her up and lifted her over the railing, dangling her until she found her footing on the hand-tied hemp ladder. As she clung to the rope, he tossed her tote bag to Tomas. Reyna cried out when she saw it fly overboard. The big man caught it with one hand and tucked it away.

"You worry too much, little one," Jules shouted from above. "Your small treasures are safe. Better you keep an eye on that emerald. It, at least, is of some value. Do whatever Tomas tells you."

He prodded Sister forward. "When you reach shore, good lady, do not be too disappointed in our resident priest."

No longer feisty, Sister Augustine held tight to the ladder, her mouth moving silently as she called down God's wrath upon the pirate ship, its captain, and crew.

When Reyna was safely seated in one of the two dugouts, Sister stepped gingerly down the ladder until her feet were at the waterline. Tomas, on the nearby raft, stretched out his big hand and held her arm until she felt stable enough to open her eyes again.

Reyna was surprised to see that the boatmen were two children—dark-skinned, dark-eyed, smiling boys who looked enough alike to be twins. They spoke back and forth to each other in a soft blurred language the girl could not identify.

Tomas came alongside in his raft. "Hold tight," he said, always sparing with his words. "Do not move about, and you," he pointed to Reyna, "pin that brooch to the inside of your dress."

He used a long pole to push the raft away from the pirate ship, leading the procession toward an inlet where fingers of marshland were scattered among rivulets of placid green water. The pirogues with their precious female cargo followed in his wake.

Reyna glanced back. Jules was silhouetted against the sky, his face shadowed, but she recognized his comic salute and, somehow, felt reassured. When Reyna turned back toward the front of her craft, she was admonished sharply by the oarsman. She didn't understand his words, but she recognized his tone. She must keep still, even her smallest movements caused the boat to rock precariously.

Within minutes, they left blue water and entered a narrow channel. Marsh grass, higher than their heads, surrounded them. Long blades leaned out and brushed against Reyna's arm. She flinched when seabirds swooped across their watery path.

The sun beat down mercilessly, its rays unbroken by any foliage. The air was close, heavy. Hundreds of serpentine waterways coiled back upon themselves. Without a guide, they would surely be lost.

The softly churning oars lulled Reyna into hypnotic slumber. Except for an occasional iridescent oily rainbow on the water surface, the colors were the monotonous creams and tans of dried grasses and reeds. Reyna faced forward, barely moving, afraid to attract the boy's wrath again. She could smell the sea and an odor of decay. Her tongue licked her lips and tasted salty grit.

Tomas's raft suddenly stopped in the water. The first pirogue jarred against it and the second one dominoed alongside. Tomas raised his hand. His silent command was strictly obeyed, except by the soft lap of water against wood and the sporadic cries of gulls on the wing.

Reyna's initial excitement turned to dread.

The nun softly demanded to know the cause of their delay. They all looked toward Tomas. Crouched on his knees on the raft, he pulled the curtain of grasses aside so he could peer to either side, slowly allowing the reeds to slip back to their original position.

Undecided, he looked back at his entourage, then raised a hand to shelter his eyes and stared off toward the seaward horizon.

Reyna followed his gaze. The sky had lost its color. Although the sun generated a brilliant light, it was set against a backdrop of pale beiges, the identical colors of the marsh. She could hardly tell where the tall grass ended and the churning clouds began as they piled one on top of the other.

What's wrong? Why have we stopped? she wondered.

Tomas ran his massive hand across his mouth and chin, then came to a decision. He pointed ahead, slowly brought a finger to his mouth in a shushing sign, and made eye contact with both passengers. Then he poled his raft out into the open water of Barataria Bay.

Chapter 9

Barataria Bay

Reyna was glad to leave the narrow marshy passage and enter the large expanse of slate-colored water. It was like drifting from one world to another. Colors changed from drab to crystalline, water from calm to bumpy, air from heavy to crisp. Out on the open water, a breeze stirred around her, cool enough to cause a shiver to ripple down her spine. In an instant, she felt alert and renewed. Reyna started to say something to Sister Augustine, but was immediately hushed by both boatmen. She looked to Tomas for an explanation.

"Sound travels across water," he whispered. "Keep quiet!"

The second boatman maneuvered his craft against Reyna's while he and his friend shared a canteen. Neither boy offered water to the passengers. Reyna took advantage of the opportunity and grasped Sister's dry, trembling fingers in a silent bond—reunited by their fear and their courage.

Barataria Bay stretched in every direction. Soon

Reyna could not determine which receding waterway was the one they'd just passed through. Despite the brisk chop of the water, the boats sped forward and soon were far from shore.

Out on the bay, Reyna could see all around her, but what she noticed first was the threatening sky. The breeze freshened. Reyna gripped the sides of the dugout tightly, her hands clawing the wood for a secure hold. The fading sun slipped behind cloud cover painted in ominous grays and rimmed by a blue-black lining. How safe would they be in these shallow boats in a storm on open water?

The ride became jolting. Raindrops splattered them. In seconds, Reyna was drenched, her beautiful dress heavy and sodden against her skin. Her teeth chattered from the chill, and her wet hair streamed in a disarrayed black mass.

Reyna looked back at the young boatman's face as he rowed steadily along, and she was relieved to see no fear written there. Sister Augustine, however, had turned to stone.

Tomas waved to the two oarsmen, who immediately brought their pirogues to either side of his raft. In no time, the big man lashed the three craft together. The boys quickly scampered onto the raft with Tomas.

Reyna wanted to be with him, too. Somehow, in the midst of a storm, his hefty frame seemed broad enough to stabilize them. But when she started to rise, intending to crawl over onto the open raft, he roared a harsh "No! On your belly!"

She didn't want to lie down in the smelly old boat. Her dress would be ruined, and she would feel so separated from the others, so alone. "Absolutely

not!'' She was defiant. "Why? I'll ruin my dress."
She looked to the nun for guidance.

Sister Augustine began to sputter protests, too.

"Down!" Tomas said. "Both of you. Do what I
say!" He stepped toward Reyna as if to force her if
she did not obey.

The women looked at each other, and not knowing
what else to do, reluctantly complied. Rain was falling in bucketfuls, and Reyna feared the pirogue
would start to fill.

She cringed as she squatted in a puddle of water.
One glance and she realized her dress was already
beyond repair. At least the gunwales of the boat
would protect her from the whipping waves. One of
the boys pulled some canvas out of a storage box in
the center of the raft and tossed a sheet over the
pirogue where Sister Augustine lay wedged, swiftly
lashing it to the stern and the bow. Then he repeated
the process on Reyna's skiff. Even though the storm
continued to rage and their stomachs were jolted by
every wave, the women, at least, were sheltered.

Reyna wrinkled her nose at the fishy smell of the
wood, taking deep breaths to hold back her nausea.
*What will Lafitte think of me now? Oh, who cares?
I'll probably drown anyway. Why did I ever under-
take this journey?*

As suddenly as the storm drenched them, it ceased
its roar and the waves smoothed out. Had the sun
reappeared? Pale glimmers of light seeped through
cracks at the bow of the boat. Reyna grew anxious
beneath the heavy canvas. She could hear the boys'
soft chatter and Tomas's deep rumble. Why didn't
they uncover her? Her dress was ruined, her hair a
mess. She needed time to get ready to meet Jean
Lafitte.

32

Chapter 10

"**A**nd what be ye carrying to Grande Terre?"
boomed a hearty but menacing voice above
Reyna. The words were friendly, yet she suspected
an implied threat.

"Supplies," Tomas answered back.

"Supplies. Ha!" The voice roared. "If I know
LeFevre, he's handpicked the best of the Spanish
booty and he's sending it ashore under your
protection."

"Aye! The man's no fool. Fine wines. A gift for
Lafitte."

"You expect me to believe there's only wine
under there."

Reyna forced herself to be as still as possible. Why
did her nose itch now? She felt a sneeze coming on.
She clinched her fists and concentrated on breathing quietly.

Tomas snarled at the stranger. "I don't care what
you think, Garbeaux. Take your hook off me raft.
Let us pass."

"I've a thirst after riding that storm. Share a bottle
or two with me, mate." The voice moved closer.

Suddenly, a knife ripped through the canvas and a frightened, cringing Reyna was revealed.

"Ah. What have we here? No doubt Lafitte will think this booty sweeter than mere wine."

The pirogue dipped, and the stranger grabbed Reyna's left arm, wrenching it behind her as he jerked her upright.

"Take your hand off the girl, *Garbage*." Tomas stepped toward the pirogue. His big hand clamped around Reyna's right arm. Garbeaux yanked her away.

Snap! Her shoulder popped out of its socket. Reyna screamed in pain.

Tomas reached for his weapon, glancing sharply toward the other pirogue that had begun to dip and sway. Sister Augustine was trying to get out from beneath the cover.

The big bald man jerked his head toward the pirogue, and one of the boys scampered onto the small boat to quiet the Sister.

"Settle down, old man. Put your cutlass away." The stranger spoke softly as he wrestled Reyna toward his skiff, his beefy hands encircling her waist.

"Garbeaux!" shouted Tomas. "I said to release her!"

The pirogue bounced in the water. Reyna fell face forward, and hit her chin. Someone stepped on her. She heard grunts, and then a loud splash.

"Scum!" roared Tomas.

The pirogue sliced through the water, towed by Tomas's raft. Reyna listened to the receding shouts of the sailor named Garbeaux—angry curses she'd never heard before, but that left little to wonder about their meaning.

34

The moving boat dipped again and she felt a light pressure on her good arm. She winced.

"Be brave," the young boatman whispered. "The storm drove us close to shore. It won't be long now."

"It hurts!" she whispered. "Hurts bad!"

"She says it hurts," he repeated to Tomas.

"The big man says Lafitte will take care of you." The boy patted her tousled hair to reassure her. Reyna stirred but found it too painful to move.

"Sister . . . ?"

"She's still hidden," he answered. "My friend is sitting on her rump to keep her still."

Reyna pictured the scene in her mind, then gratefully slipped into star-studded oblivion.

∽∾∽

Chapter 11

Grand Terre

Sister Augustine, first on shore, was indignant. She stood on the wobbly pier, hands on her hips, shoulders squared, ready to do battle with Tomas. But he ignored her.

When Reyna's boat was brought alongside, the nun looked down on the inert girl and was shocked by her condition. She knew there'd been some kind of altercation at sea. The boatman had been so insulting as to sit on her to keep her still. Sister knew it was for her own good, but his actions were inappropriate, especially toward a bride of the church.

"Reyna! What's wrong with her?" she demanded. "Is she hurt? Who did this?"

"Quiet!" Tomas retrieved Reyna from the pirogue.

She groaned. One eyelid opened. She recognized Sister, then slipped back into semiconsciousness.

Sister Augustine surveyed the damage. Reyna's black hair was curled in damp ringlets, her face was smudged with dirt and tears, a bloody scrape marred her chin, and her beautiful dress was stained the color of mud.

Tomas gently placed Reyna on the wooden dock. He spat foreign words that sent the two boys scampering into the surrounding palmetto thickets.

Opposite Tomas, Sister slipped to her knees beside Reyna and watched him take a small dagger from his waistband and insert it into the cuff of the girl's sleeve.

"What are you doing?" she demanded. At his reproachful stare, she sat in silence and watched him rip the material from wrist to neckline. He peeled the fabric back to expose Reyna's battered shoulder.

Gingerly, he ran his fingers across Reyna's collarbone, then probed at her left shoulder socket and felt down her arm. Reyna stirred and whimpered but did not wake.

"Is it broken?" Sister asked.

"Aye. There's damage."

A rustling sound announced the return of the two boys, who carried between them a makeshift stretcher—a colorful woven blanket wrapped around two long poles. Several villagers accompanied them.

Tomas directed two of the men to hold the stretcher while he gently placed Reyna on it. A woman gave him her shawl, which he folded into a thick square and placed beneath the hurt shoulder.

The woman made the sign of the cross, then tentatively nudged Sister Augustine's arm. Sister balked. Tomas was their caretaker, but he was still ignoring her. He seemed more interested in directing the boys about where to hide the watercraft. Reyna was hurt and had already been carried out of sight. And here this strange woman was tugging at her, trying to lead her away in another direction.

The woman wore high-top boots, men's brown britches, and a very low-cut red blouse that exposed much of her bosom. *No wonder she needs a stole,* the nun thought unkindly.

"Come, I will take care of you. My name is Cara." The woman slipped her arm into the crook of Sister Augustine's arm and gently urged her forward.

"Where are they taking the child?" Sister asked, walking uncomfortably arm-in-arm with the woman.

"To the house of Jean Lafitte. His mistress, Catherine, has healing hands. What is your story, Holy One? What brings you here?"

"I was escorting the girl to New Orleans. These . . . these villains attacked our ship and killed the crew. We were forced into these tiny boats. A terrible storm hit and then a man named Garbeaux . . ."

"Ah, Garbeaux, he's a bad one."

"He hurt Reyna. I couldn't see. They covered me to keep off the rain. I'm afraid for the girl."

"Do not worry," Cara said. "We may be a village of pirates—Lafitte prefers the name 'corsair'—but we are not as cruel as the world makes us out to be."

The two women continued through thick undergrowth until they came to a clearing. Dwarf oak trees were scattered all about and leaned in only one direction, away from the sea. *Odd trees,* Sister thought, *with such gnarled and twisted trunks.* They grew in dense groves, hiding the small houses clustered beneath their branches.

Each house had its own thicket of shrubs to protect it from the Gulf wind. Sister Augustine noticed its bite for the first time and shivered.

Chapter 12

"**C**ome to my house," Cara said. "I'll find you something to wear while we wash your garments. You'll want to be dressed properly when you meet Lafitte and Father Francis."

"No! What I have on will do nicely until I see Reyna. I must protect her. She is my ward."

"She's in good hands," the woman said, then hesitated. "I do not wish to presume, but, Sister, surely you would have more authority if you were dry and wearing clean vestments. As you are now, I'm not sure anyone will pay attention to you. Look at yourself."

Sister Augustine took inventory. Her brown habit was soiled with mud and she wrinkled her nose at the fishy smell that clung to it. The white guimpe that framed her face and formed a collar was dingy and stained. She felt her face and rubbed away droplets of mud that stuck there. Her mouth tasted of grit.

"You may be right, Cara, but I'm very concerned about Reyna. Would you go and seek news of her?"

"I'll send my daughter, Gabriella. She is favored at Lafitte's house. Here. This way." She tugged on

Sister's arm, leading her down a dirt path toward the water and several palm trees.

They entered a squatty house containing only two rooms. The windows were covered with heavy shades, battened securely to the window frame, and the roof was palmetto thatch. Sunlight streamed in through cracks in the rough-made brick and mud walls, leaving odd patterns to dance across the bare floorboards. Motes of dust floated in the air. There was little furniture, except for a magnificent cherry étagère, probably looted from some captured ship, and a handmade wooden table shoved against a wall in the primitive kitchen. Three beds, built of cedar posts and stretched cowhide, lined the back wall of the other room.

Cara suddenly seemed embarrassed. "It doesn't look like much, but it's my home. Welcome."

Sister fingered the rough material of her habit and the mud-splattered belted scapular hanging over her tunic. Her veil was so torn, it could not be repaired. "Where will you wash my clothes?"

"Outside." Cara pulled the shade away from the window so Sister Augustine could peer out. A wash-tub rested on a tree stump, and a clothesline dangled from two limbs. A smoldering campfire burned nearby.

"The wind off the water will dry your things quickly. Let me find you something else to put on."

Sister Augustine stood in the middle of the bedroom, feeling very exposed. When she began to disrobe, every noise startled her, and she froze. "Where is your husband?" she asked.

"Oh, he is with LeFevre. Picou is a good man. Surely you met him. He is second in command."

"Yes," Sister answered. "We met. He frightened

me. But I could see he still held some regard for the Mother Church."

"Oh, don't mind him. He loves to tease." When Cara returned, her arms were laden with dresses. "Surely one of these will fit." She unfolded undergarments, as well as beautiful velvet and brocade gowns, too rich for Sister Augustine's simple tastes.

"Where did these come from?" Sister knew full well the answer.

"Picou likes to bring me dresses. But I prefer something more casual." Cara indicated the clothes she was wearing. "I pick and choose, keep what I want, and store the rest. The material comes in handy." She shrugged.

"I had a valise . . ."

"Tomas will bring it. Here, give me your things. I want you to look saintly when you go to meet Lafitte."

"Wait," the Sister ordered. "My Rosary, in the pocket."

Cara handed her the prayer beads, then left the room humming a lilting melody. A few moments later, Cara returned with a bucket of sun-warmed water for bathing.

After washing and dressing, Sister surveyed the bedroom and was instantly drawn to one wall, where, hanging from a nail, she found an elaborate crucifix of gold with a ruby inserted at its center.

Reverently, the nun took it down, and carried it next to her heart to a spot in the center of the bedroom. There the rays of the waning sun met in a splash of warmth and light. She slipped to her knees, the crucifix clutched to her bosom, and began to pray.

Chapter 13

Reyna felt herself being lifted from the swaying stretcher and placed on a clean, linen-covered bed, and she cried out when her shoulder bumped against the lumpy moss-packed mattress. Her eyes opened wide at the sight of the man and the girl who studied her from the foot of the four-poster. The girl wasn't much older than she.

Because her shoulder hurt badly, she soon lost interest in the strangers. It didn't matter who they were as long as they could alleviate the pain. The man issued orders, "Clean her up. If the damage is too much for you to handle, Catherine, then send for a physician from the mainland."

Reyna stared at him. He was the most handsome man she had ever seen. He was tall, taller than Jules, with dark liquid eyes and pale skin. His face was clean-shaven, except for sideburns that grew partway down his cheeks. He smiled at her and patted the mattress.

"Do not fret, little one. I am Jean Lafitte. You are safe here. My Catherine will take good care of you. Your friend is with Picou's wife, Cara, a good woman. She will rejoin you when she has had time to rest." His smile disappeared. "I must leave you now. I have business with Garbeaux."

His dark eyes flashed from Reyna to Catherine. He gave a curt nod, and left the room. Tomas, who was standing at the doorway, saluted the two women, then followed Lafitte.

When the men were gone, Catherine gently touched Reyna's tear-stained cheek. Then she turned Reyna's head so that she would have to look at her. "Jean Lafitte welcomes you to his home," she said. "I am Catherine."

Reyna swallowed. The throb in her shoulder had slowly taken possession of her entire body and she could feel herself drifting. She wanted to say something. What was it? She closed her eyes, then forced them open. "I . . . I am afraid."

Catherine turned slightly away. When she swung back, she was holding a cloth soaked with warm almond-scented water. Gently, she smoothed it over Reyna's forehead, down her cheeks, across her mouth, and then swabbed at her neck.

"Your dress is ruined," Catherine said. "I must remove it. Lie still and let me do the work."

It was too much effort to speak, so Reyna simply blinked her eyes in agreement.

Catherine used snips to cut the dress from Reyna's upper body. She was stronger than she looked. She lifted Reyna away from the pillows, and peeled the dress as far down as it would go. Then, with one arm wedged under Reyna's lower back, Catherine shimmied the rest of the garment down to the foot of the bed, dropping it into a soiled heap on the floor.

Using a washcloth and heated water, she bathed Reyna gently, then lifted her into a sitting position.

Catherine then placed the girl's good arm into the sleeve of a wine-colored silk robe. She pulled it around Reyna, behind and in front, leaving the damaged shoulder and arm exposed. She pinned the fabric closed at the bodice, then belted and tied the robe at Reyna's slender waist.

Reyna slumped against the pillows and thanked Catherine with a pained smile.

"I know if I were in the house of strangers," Catherine said, "I would want to be taken care of this way. Now I must look at your injury. I will try not to hurt you."

"Is it broken?" Reyna said in a whimper.

Catherine shook her head as she felt along the girl's collarbone until she reached the shoulder socket. Reyna winced, but held back a scream.

"Your shoulder may be dislocated," Catherine said. "It will hurt when we pop it back into place, but it must be done. Then it will heal quickly and you will again have full use of your arm."

"When . . . when will you do it?"

"It should be done now. Immediately. Tomas is guarding us. You trust him, don't you?"

Reyna nodded. "I guess so." Her voice was weak, even to her own ears.

"Wait here," Catherine said, then disappeared into the next room.

Where would I go? Reyna thought.

Tomas returned with Catherine, and looked down upon Reyna from his six-foot plus height. Light from the kerosene lamp glinted off his bald dome. "I did not take very good care of you," he said. "I am sorry."

Catherine patted the big man's arm. "I will tell

Jean and Jules how you helped me put the shoulder back.''

The huge man grimaced. ''Close your eyes,'' he said gruffly. He took Reyna's arm in one hand, her shoulder in the other and with firm pressure and a quick twist, he inserted the shoulder bone back into its socket.

Reyna screamed. Her nails gouged into Tomas's arm, drawing blood. Mercifully, she fainted.

Chapter 14

Reyna awoke to bright sunlight, streaming in through double doors that opened onto a terrace overlooking a ribbon of beach. Her left arm was bound to her body with clean, soft rags, and she was wearing the silk robe Catherine had given her the night before.

Was her light-headedness due to the spoonfuls of medicine fed to her throughout the long night? It felt good to lie still, to soak up the sun, and to forget for a moment that she was the captive of pirates.

But the peaceful quiet did not last long. Reyna heard shouts and she could see the shadow of someone pacing on the balcony outside her door. She managed to sit on the side of the bed, but it took a moment to regain her equilibrium. Her shoulder ached dully, and there was a soft roar inside her head.

Who is shouting? she wondered. *Could it be the handsome man from the night before—the infamous Jean Lafitte?*

"Garbeaux, come forth!" the man yelled again. "Do not hide like a weasel behind your men. I demand an explanation."

Reyna slipped bare feet onto the wooden floor and tiptoed to the open doorway. Woozy, she clung to the door frame to keep from falling. It occurred to her that someone might think she was eavesdropping, but she didn't have the strength now to make it back to the bed.

From where she was hidden, she could hear and see everything, and she would be safe . . . unless Jean Lafitte turned around and saw her.

A man, standing on the ground below the terrace, held his hat in his hands at his belly. He wore a dark navy waistcoat and soiled white britches. His pose was one of submission, but his eyes flashed angry sparks.

"I did nothing wrong!" he shouted at Lafitte. "Your own man, Jules LeFevre, is the one you should be chastising. Tomas sneaked the girl ashore. Claimed the pirogue was laden with fine wine. I figured he was taking his share and yours before the rest of us even knew it existed. I thought our rule was 'Share and share alike'."

Garbeaux nodded at the other crew members who had gathered in the clearing below Lafitte's house.

Is Garbeaux inciting a rebellion?

"Jules was acting under my orders," Lafitte answered.

"Your orders!" Garbeaux spat upon the crushed oyster shell that paved the clearing. "Who elected you our leader?" Several of Garbeaux's men nodded in agreement. A wave of muttering sifted through the crowd.

"We have a council, Garbeaux. And you are not one of the ten who rule Grand Terre. Our rule is to share, yes," Lafitte said, "but if we harm this girl or the Catholic nun who accompanies her, we are

47

immediately in line for retribution from Governor Claiborne. I do not wish to bring that kind of trouble down upon our heads. Besides, fine ransoms are not paid for damaged goods."

"I did nothing wrong," Garbeaux whined in his own defense.

"Your intention was to take the girl for your own. In the process, she was hurt."

Garbeaux spoke under his breath, which resulted in snickers from several of his followers. Reyna shivered when she realized she was the subject of this fierce harangue. Suddenly she felt the air stir behind her. She shrank away from the doorway to face Catherine.

For the first time, she recognized the beauty of the golden-skinned girl. Catherine wore a simple but elegant dress of damask. A huge teardrop pearl hung in the hollow of her throat. Her dark hair was piled high on her head. Slender. Exotic. Skin creamy and smooth. Brown eyes sober but friendly.

Catherine slipped an arm around Reyna's waist and pulled her close so that she could rest her slight weight against Catherine's body.

"It scares me when they act like this," Catherine whispered. "So angry, so greedy. All these little banty roosters. Jean will never give in to Garbeaux. He would rather die."

Reyna's dark eyes darted back and forth between the man standing in the clearing and Lafitte above him at the terrace railing.

Lafitte pronounced the punishment. "You will pay a fee to the treasury for the damage you have done to this prize. The council will decide how much." When he turned to leave, his dark eyes casually raked over the two young women hovering inside the doorway.

Reyna's quick intake of breath warned him just as Catherine screamed out, "No-o-o-o . . ."

Lafitte whirled around, his hand already reaching for his pistol. In one smooth movement, he swiftly drew it from his belt, pointed, and fired. Blue flame billowed from the muzzle.

Lafitte's bullet entered the man's left shoulder, shattering the socket—the identical place where Reyna had been hurt. The gun Garbeaux had concealed beneath his hat flew in an arc away from his body. The pirate crumpled to the ground, writhing in pain, reduced to a crying hulk.

Smoke curled from the barrel of Lafitte's gun. The men in the yard stood frozen for what seemed like a very long moment.

"Do any of you disagree with what has taken place here today?" Lafitte's voice was cold, deadly. He pulled a second pistol from his waistband and held it aloft.

The men wandered off in small groups while two of Garbeaux's followers hefted the injured man and carried him away.

"Alligator bait. Good for nothing!" Lafitte removed his hat, dipped his head and planted an affectionate buss on Catherine's cheek. He tilted Reyna's head back with a finger under her chin so that she had to look up at him.

"And, you, my dear Reyna," he said, "how are you today?"

Chapter 15

That afternoon, Sister Augustine's pleas to see Reyna were finally answered, and she was ushered into the airy upstairs bedroom of Jean Lafitte's home. She found Reyna reclined in a red hammock, shaded by the eaves of the tiled roof. She was wearing one of her own dresses, and the only indication she had been injured was that she held her left arm close to her body.

"I'd get up," Reyna said lazily, "but I'm not sure I can. Isn't this heaven?" She waved toward the Gulf and the narrow sandy beach.

"Heaven, indeed! Looks like you're mending." Sister Augustine spoke through clenched teeth. Here was Reyna, comfortable and rested, while she, worried sick about the girl's well-being, ached from her sleepless night on a cowhide cot

"Aye," Reyna answered, then covered her mouth to smother the giggle that erupted when she used the pirate word for yes.

"Don't get too comfortable. I've seen how women are treated in this place. Aye, and I've met their Friar Tuck. I can tell you right now, the priest, father Francis he's called, does not care a fare-thee-well for me. He said they'd no need of my 'meddling'!'' The nun folded her arms across her chest.

Reyna struggled to sit up in the hammock. She swung her legs over the side and gained the floor. Tentatively, she placed her hand on the nun's shoulder. "I'm sorry, Sister," she said. "I know these past few days have not been easy for you."

Sister Augustine stifled a sob. "I thought I stood up pretty well to the pirates on the ship, and I survived that wild rainstorm on the bay. Picou's wife, Cara, took me in. But, child, they kept me from tending to you, and then that malevolent priest told me I wasn't wanted here. I feel so useless, yes, and old." She crumpled into a throne-like wicker chair and batted back her tears.

"Oh, it's not that bad." Reyna attempted to cheer her. "Jean Lafitte is very kind, and Catherine is a delight. We're already friends. Why, do you know we're the same age?"

Reyna wandered over to the railing and looked out at the huts nestled under the twisted oak trees, then searched the sky and water. "I feel at peace here. My arm is better already. And Catherine has assured me there's plenty of work at Jean's house. She said I can live here."

"What of the man to whom you are promised?"

"What of him? He will never find me in this backwater swamp. Granted, he may look for a while, but when he can't find me, he'll give me up for dead. That's what Catherine said."

"And what of me?" For the first time, Sister Augustine slumped in defeat.

"You are very much needed here," Lafitte answered from a place near the French doors. He

51

walked over to the nun, bowed, and proffered his hand. Sister Augustine, flustered by his gentlemanly conduct, did not offer hers in return. "Yes, you are very much needed here," he repeated. "I hope you will agree to stay."

"Do I have a choice?" She started to rise.

"Stay seated, dear lady." Lafitte knelt on one knee before her

"I do not want either of you to think of yourselves as prisoners. It is a misfortune that your trip was interrupted, but we must believe there is a grander purpose. You, dear Sister, will be used of God here in this isolated little backwater swamp, as Reyna so charmingly describes my home. And Reyna, beautiful Reyna, may be more suited for the elegant life of New Orleans than a dreary ranch in godforsaken Tejas."

He stood and gestured with a sweep of his hand. "The entire island is yours. You are free to go wherever you like. Keep in mind that all of my men are not gentlemen, and that alligators and snakes infest these waters. Stay on high ground, and do not wander off alone."

The nun wrestled herself out of the chair. Her bones creaked, and every muscle was stiff from her restless night. "Where will I live if Reyna stays here? And can you assure me of her safety, that neither you nor any of your men will take advantage of her innocence? There's also the matter of how I can serve anyone, if the priest doesn't want me here."

"Ah!" He chuckled. "You've made the acquaintance of Father Francis, I see. You'll like him when you get to know him. I'll tell him to give you free rein with the women. He's a little brusque, but he advises me on things of a higher nature, and I am constantly amazed at his wisdom.''

"Does his wisdom come from the bottle he seems to keep firmly planted at his lips?''

The nun's scorn caused Lafitte's bushy eyebrows to rise. Laugh lines crinkled in the outer corners of his dark brown eyes.

"You will have to learn that for yourself. You asked about Reyna's safety and your own living arrangements. Reyna is a prize, and like any treasure, she will be protected. At this moment, some of the women are preparing a vacant cottage for you, near the chapel.'' The pirate turned and pointed at a thatched roof situated off to itself in a grove of orange trees. "Garbeaux and his followers will no longer need it.''

Sister crossed herself and started to say something about the violence of the morning, but Reyna shook her head in warning.

"Reyna, my dear, if you feel well enough, accompany the Sister to her cottage. Help her make it more livable. But do not tax your strength. Mind you, the medicine Catherine gave you could cause you to faint. Later, the two of you may want to visit our chapel.''

Lafitte dismissed them abruptly and swung into the newly vacated hammock. The girl and the nun held hands as they descended the outside staircase and hastened toward Sister's new home.

∽∽∽

Chapter 16

Bayou near Grand Terre

Benito Sandoval's oar dipped silently into the still green waters as he and his guide floated gently toward the bank. The air seemed close and fetid. Birds and insects dispensed a steady hum of screeches and chirps and, just ahead of them, a fat alligator waddled toward the water, his powerful tail slapping at the mud. The creature glided toward the center of the bayou, then turned around to study the small boat.

"Mean and ugly! I hope he's not looking for dinner," Benito's words were cut short by the slashing sign made by his guide. The man raised a finger to his lips. Benito swallowed the lump in his throat that always appeared when battle was imminent.

His guide was a cranky Cajun with a thick accent and a sturdy body stained dark brown by the harsh southern sun. He eased them toward the bank by tugging on supple willow limbs, and tied the boat to a cypress knot. He pulled his gun out of his waistband, then stepped ashore.

Benito left his leather hat balanced on the oarlock, and followed him onto the gummy earth that mired his every footstep. He, too, drew his weapon.

"This way." The guide motioned and pointed ahead through the dense swamp. "Their settlement is just on the other side of this slough. Watch for moccasins."

A mosquito dived into Benito's ear and, without thinking, he slapped at it, the noise uncommonly loud in the silence of the moss-laden cypress trees. The guide frowned at the mestizo. Benito gestured to assure him he would be quieter.

On the alert, they high-stepped through the quagmire, and finally reached a place where the winter sun filtered through the mossy umbrella. The guide knelt and parted a curtain of reeds and grasses. They could see evidence of a village on the other side of a narrow channel. Smokey fires dotted the landscape. Benito glanced at his pocket watch. It was four o'clock. It would be dark in a few hours.

"How do we get across?" he whispered.

"We wade. Better you worry about how we get back."

"I just want to make sure the girl and the nun are here. Then we'll get help."

The Cajun crossed himself.

They slashed down tall fronds of grasses, which they held in front of them as they made their way slowly across the shallow waterway.

When they neared land, Benito caught the Cajun's arm and held him back so that he could go first. The guide silently shook his head in disgust.

Hatless, in a crouch, with gun drawn, Benito advanced up a cobbled pathway. His pants clung wetly to his legs, and his boots were so weighted with mud he felt slightly off balance. His eyes were not on his feet, so he didn't see the tautly strung line that lay across his path. It was connected to a network of fishing lines leading to overhead branches in a nearby tree. The tree limbs dipped. Nesting birds flew into a frenzy, screeching an alarm as they soared out of the treetops.

"*Sacre bleu!* Let's get out of here." The guide plunged back toward the water. Benito, undecided, wanted at least one good look at the village so he moved forward up the slight incline.

At the top, he was bowled over by a huge bald man who leaped on him and pinned him beneath his bulk. The large pirate cursed as he clumsily tried to get to his cutlass. Frightened, Benito fired his gun. The pirate slumped on top of him, a deadweight. Benito panicked. *I must get free!*

He could hear men shouting and crashing toward him. He pushed with all of his might, and heaved the body off of him. Free, he took one step, but the man's massive hand grabbed his ankle and jerked him down. Benito pulled out of the grasp, scrambled a short distance on his knees, then turned back to look into the man's glazing eyes. He knew he had to hurry. The Cajun guide, an unknown, was nowhere to be seen. He might leave Benito there to die.

Benito wanted to run. But he hadn't learned what he needed to know. *Is the girl here? Is she safe?*

He crawled over to the wounded pirate, and pressed the man's own knife to his throat. Benito growled, "Is Reyna here? Do you have her, you bloodthirsty dog!"

Tomas lifted his head an inch and spat at his assailant. "Aye, we have her. And we be keepin' her."

His eyes rolled back and his head thudded against the ground.

Benito dodged off the path, leaping over cypress roots and brushing low-hanging moss out of his face as he ran.

A bullet whizzed past his ear. Another one tore into his upper right arm. His gun dropped to the ground for he had no feeling in his hand.

With his free hand, Benito grabbed his arm tightly to stem the flow of blood, and bounded toward where they'd left the boat. Every step jarred him.

"If that . . . left me high and dry . . . *te mato* . . . I'll kill him." He stomped through the palmettoes, landing on his knees in the mud beside the canoe.

The Cajun guide half-lifted him into the boat, pushed off from the muddy bank, and paddled like a madman toward the bayou's bend. Benito heard the curses of the men left behind. His lips curved in a satisfied smile when several big gators parted the green water heading toward shore. His pursuers would have to turn back.

Chapter 17

New Orleans

Compadre, Benito wrote.

> *Reyna has been captured by Jean Lafitte's pirates and is being held at their camp in Barataria. I do not know her condition, nor that of the Catholic nun. The governor here is mounting a drive against the man. He has already arrested his brother, Pierre, who lays wait in a New Orleans jail, expecting to be rescued.*
>
> *My wound prevents me from joining the militia when it attacks Grand Terre. I am leaving word that you should be contacted as soon as Reyna or the nun surfaces. I hope they grind these insects into the stinking mud that surrounds their village.*
>
> *I am on my way home. I regret I cannot send you any good news.*
>
> *Your servant, Benito*

Chapter 18

Summary, 1814

Reyna and Sister Augustine quickly fell into step with life on Grande Terre. For a time, the village buzzed with rumors about the man who killed Tomas, how he might come back with soldiers, and how the entire settlement could be in serious danger—especially now that Pierre had been jailed. But all was quiet.

Reyna helped in the big house and became a close companion to Catherine. Lafitte, always courteous, seldom acknowledged Reyna, his mind occupied by graver matters, such as survival, Catherine said.

The two young women shared chores and confidences, too. Reyna learned that Catherine's sister, Marie Villar, was the matchmaker who introduced her to the handsome pirate. Marie and Jean's brother, Pierre, had been involved romantically for a number of years.

"It is a man's world," Catherine explained. "We quadroon women rely on wealthy men to take care of us. We are taught, from an early age, how to

59

please the rich and powerful gentlemen of our world. We remain chaste, we dress modestly. You see, it is better for me to be a mistress, than to live by my wits in New Orleans.''

Catherine told Reyna she had loved Jean since childhood. In her heart, she knew he was the only man for her.

Some day, will there be a man like Jean for me? Reyna wondered.

Maybe it would be the handsome rogue, Jules Le-Fevre, who boldly stared at her whenever they were together. Many times he had asked her to dance—but Sister Augustine always interfered and harshly admonished Reyna about remaining pure.

Reyna could not help but be aware that she was growing more beautiful with every sunrise, and she also knew she was safe, as long as she lived under Jean Lafitte's roof.

Reyna made a point to speak little but listen a lot, except when the talk was political. Then she closed her ears, for she was far more interested in romantic tales of the sea and pirate lore

Meanwhile, Sister Augustine rolled up her sleeves and began a campaign to improve living conditions on the island. The nun and Father Francis called an uneasy truce.

Sister insisted that her cottage be whitewashed inside and out. She swept the wooden floors and dusted the rafters. She set a table with Lafitte's best china, and kept a kettle simmering on hot coals should guests drop by.

In daytime, she taught Bible stories to the island's youngsters. In the afternoon, she held classes on child care, homemaking, and hygiene.

At eventide, she often sat outdoors and waited for

the women to file by—some by themselves, others in small groups. They talked of their lives, their fears, their dreams. Sister Augustine offered advice based on Christian principles.

To Father Francis's surprise, he was asked to officiate at a number of weddings and baptisms. Mass no longer was attended by mostly females, and even some of the men asked for the rite of confession. A few pirates removed their families from the island and headed for New Orleans to make an honest living.

One day, the priest patted Sister's arm to get her full attention. He rubbed his nose, until he finally seemed ready to speak. "Sister, I never would have thought it possible, but your work here is paying off for our Lord. I see a unity among the men and women, a family setting for the children. I've seen some of the worst plunderers take their women by the hand in quiet walks, and even play with their offspring. That is a glorious sight!"

He hesitated. "You're doing a wonderful job here. I already have reported it to the bishop."

"Thank you, Father." Sister bowed her head in humility, then boldly stared at him through pleading eyes. "Everywhere I look, I see more to do. We need a school, and a physician in residence, and ..."

Father Francis raised his hands to ward off her words. "Enough. Enough, woman!" His smile belied his tone of exasperation. "Take it slow. One step at a time. We must take care not to irritate our masters."

One sweltering summer evening at dusk, Reyna and Sister Augustine rested outside the nun's whitewashed cottage, sitting in ornately carved highbacked chairs befitting a king's palace. On several occasions, they had discussed how extravagantly expensive furniture, jewels, and clothing seemed to diminish in value upon reaching Grand Terre.

The very same items would bring enormous prices in auctions at The Temple—the platform Lafitte's men had hid deep in the marshes. It was there the pirates displayed their contraband merchandise when they weren't brazen enough to show it in a New Orleans back alley

The Temple was near enough to the city for buyers to come in droves, snapping up slaves and stolen treasures to resell or keep. The pirates were pleased by the riches resulting from the sale of contraband, but on Grand Terre, a chair was a chair.

Reyna lifted her long dark hair off the back of her neck. When it fell again to her shoulders, she leaned forward to blow little puffs of air into the inner reaches of her cotton blouse. "It is so hot," she said. "I wish for rain."

"From the looks of those thunderclouds over there, you may get your wish." Sister Augustine poured them another glass of lemon-flavored water, then slumped, her head resting against the chair's tall back

"Ah, this is good," Reyna said

"My child," Sister Augustine said, "lemons are a rarity. We have them only because the pirates attacked a vessel from South America. A bushel of lemons is worth how many lives, do you think?" The woman's face reflected the war that raged inside of her. Of late, she had said many things to Reyna that expressed a growing discontent with Lafitte and his pirates. The girl hoped the nun would not complain too loudly.

Sister looks drained, Reyna thought. *The moist*

heat here is all-consuming. The girl drank deeply again, and wished for something to say that would bring animation back to Sister's face. "Did you know, that last year at this time, Jean was a wanted man? I heard them laughing about it at a card game last night."

Sister raised her eyebrows. "He still is." Her tone was matter-of-fact.

"But this is a funny story," Reyna said. "The governor posted an arrest warrant for Jean last summer. It was after a company of dragoons found the pirates with a shipload of contraband goods. There was a fight. One of the Americans was wounded."

"My dear," Sister Augustine interrupted, "how can this be funny to you? Lafitte is a murderer, a thief. We are here under his protection, but do not forget what manner of man he is."

"You don't understand," Reyna continued. "What's funny is that the governor's arrest warrant was posted in public places all over New Orleans. Jean went into the city the very next day, and no one treated him any differently. He stood out in the open and read the wanted poster, and laughed out-right . . ."

"I still don't see . . ."

"Two days later, a similar arrest warrant appeared in the same places—but this one offered a reward for the arrest of the governor. The paper was signed by Jean Lafitte. The pirates laughed and laughed."

Sister Augustine's voice grew ominous. "A cover-up for their fear. I'm told Lafitte's empire could fall."

Reyna leaned forward, surprised Sister Augustine was privy to such information. "Tell me," she said, "what have you heard?"

"Well, my dear, it seems we came to America in the middle of a war with England. Somehow the importance of that escaped me. Napoleon has been fighting his way across Europe, and the United States and Britain are at war over here. The English Navy threatens the entire coastline . . ."

"I didn't know . . ." said Reyna. "What is it all about?"

"As I understand it, British warships seized American merchant ships and searched them for British subjects. Whenever they found one, they forced him to serve in the British Navy, because of the war with France. Sometimes they took Americans by mistake. And this made the citizens of this upstart nation very angry."

"Well, I can understand that, but . . ." said Reyna.

"Oh, there's more," Sister continued. "The British have encouraged Indians to go on the warpath, giving them guns and gun powder. The Indians have attacked American forts, hoping to keep white settlers from taking more of their lands. Slaves have escaped from plantations and joined the Indians. Unrest is everywhere."

"What does any of this have to do with Jean?"

"The Americans have decided to no longer abide the crimes committed by Lafitte and his men. They are out for blood. They will neither bow before England, their mother nation, nor before a murderous scamp such as Jean Lafitte."

"Are we in danger?"

"Who knows?" Sister shrugged. "You and I may be safer here in this swamp than anywhere else— except Tejas."

Reyna sighed. "I've often wondered if the man who shot Tomas was sent by Don Carlos."

"At any rate, if he does come back, he may have to hunt for us. We may not be here," Sister said.

"Where would we go?"

"The swamps, I suppose. I've heard Lafitte is already preparing to disappear. His brother is in jail, in chains. And, again, there is this price on Lafitte's head. Father Francis warned me that the Americans want to destroy the Temple, and they want to crush the pirates, too."

"Will they come after him here?"

"I expect they will, if they want him bad enough."

A weariness seemed to overcome the nun. "Our little voyage to the Americas has placed us in much jeopardy. Stay alert, Reyna. Our lives are definitely at risk."

Chapter 19

September 1814

As usual, Reyna was up ahead of the sun to see that bread was freshly baked and coffee boiled for the Lafitte household. She poured herself a demitasse of the dark thick liquid. A loud explosion shook the house, and hot coffee spilled down the front of her thin nightdress, scalding her. Holding the wet gown away from her body, she bit her lower lip to keep from crying.

Pain was forgotten when Lafitte bounded down the stairs two at a time, dressing as he ran. Before the echo died away, she heard shouts and curses from outside. Reyna stepped into a clearing near the house and was almost knocked down as Lafitte's men raced toward the beach. Some brandished pistols, others waved cutlasses over their heads. Everyone screamed, but the words were indistinguishable.

To Reyna, it looked as if hundreds of angry hornets were swarming headlong and mindless in the direction of the cannon fire.

Catherine suddenly appeared at her side and

handed her a shawl to cover her cotton gown. "Go to Sister Augustine. Bring her back here. Jean thinks we are being invaded."

"By whom?" Reyna asked.

"He is not sure. We have so many enemies."

Reyna dashed to Sister's cottage, but it was empty. Where could she be? *The chapel? Of course.* The pealing of the newly installed church bell had hardly registered. Reyna joined other women flocking toward the church and found Sister relinquishing her hold on the bellpull to two young boys.

Sister Augustine and Reyna hugged, then stood with their arms around each other as they watched the action on the beach.

A British brig-of-war came into full view. Lafitte jumped in a small boat, ordering four armed men to row him out to a pass between two islands. As soon as Lafitte's boat appeared in the pass, a dinghy darted away from the larger vessel and bore down upon Lafitte and his men.

"Reyna, get the spyglass from inside the church," Sister ordered. "Tell me what you see."

Reyna complied. "Three officers are on the small boat. Two are dressed in naval uniforms and one wears a scarlet military jacket. A white flag waves from the bow, a British unionjack from the stern."

"Our men . . . on the beach . . . ?" cried one of the women. Focus shifted back to Grand Terre's waterfront where several boatloads of heavily armed pirates pushed out into the waves. Women and children watched from afar as Lafitte made frantic gestures, warning his men to stay back.

Catherine slipped next to Reyna, visibly shaken, tears trickling down her cheeks. "What's happening?"

"Here's the spyglass," Reyna said. "Take a look."

"No, I am afraid," Catherine said. "I am afraid we are under siege by the British." She patted the waistband of her skirt where a single-shot pistol was wedged into place. "Jean told me President Madison had to run for his life. The First Lady, Dolly, barely saved the Declaration of Independence. She ran for safety with it under her arm, while the British fired on Washington."

Catherine gulped air. "Jean has been so tense lately. Our friends warned us of English warships in the Gulf of Mexico. And the Americans, they want him, too." Catherine clutched at Sister Augustine. "Dear Sister, pray for Jean. Pray for his safety."

Sister Augustine gathered together the bedraggled group of women. No one drew a weapon at the meeting in the middle of the channel. So, like a mother hen, Sister hustled the women into the chapel to pray.

"Let us seek holy protection." Sister's firm voice seemed too loud in the stillness of the chapel.

Reyna slipped to her knees. *A British warship at our front door. Angry Americans breathing fire and brimstone down our backs. How will it end?*

Chapter 20

After meeting the British in the middle of the channel, Jean Lafitte gathered his officers at his home. As unobtrusive as possible, Reyna filled their mugs with thick black coffee and lingered within call. She intended to eavesdrop, but it was not necessary for their voices quickly rose in loud disagreement.

"Quiet now, we haven't much time," Jean ordered. "They arrive in a few minutes. It may not be necessary for us to fight the British. They probably want us to join them against the Americans. I have to tell you, my sympathies lie with the people here— not with those across the sea. I am a Frenchman. The British will always be my enemy."

"Is that wise?" Picou asked. "The English Navy is the finest in the world. What chance do these planters and merchants have against such power? I say we join the Brits. We certainly can't beat them."

Lafitte clapped Picou on the back. "My fiery friend, the scent of battle is in your nostrils. To my thinking, you don't really care whose side you're on, as long as you get to fight."

The atmosphere seemed lighter after his small joke, and Reyna marveled at how easily Jean maneuvered the moods of his followers.

Jules, whose chair was tilted against the wall, spoke for the first time. "Aye, you may be right about Picou. Not one of us has ever run from a fight." The chair's front legs clattered to the stone floor when he stood. "I say let's wait and see what they want. You invited them ashore, so let's entertain them. Ply them with brandy and every delicacy in our stores. Let the Brits see a wealthy and mighty community here. I'll see that our men are armed. We can even roll out a cannon or two. They'll think twice about attacking such a strong fortress."

"No, Jules," Lafitte said. "Let Picou take care of distributing weapons. I want you on the beach to welcome them. You have a way with words."

The two pirates chortled and left the room. Jean snapped his fingers for Reyna and Catherine, and he issued orders regarding the elaborate breakfast to be prepared for his guests.

Within the hour, Jean Lafitte and Jules LeFevre were leading three British officers on a lengthy roundabout tour of the island, allowing time for the pirate women to prepare a gigantic morning meal. Only Reyna and Catherine had been told it was Jean's intention to glut the British as a delaying tactic.

Island women raided the storerooms and created a feast. Loaves of baked breads and pastries, trays of tropical fruits, platters of fish, shrimp, crab and crawfish, even fried alligator. They served smoked venison and beef, bowls of rice, and summer vegetables. Picou uncorked vintage wines of Spain and France.

The meal, which started around nine o'clock, was

served on a long table in Jean's living room. Shutters were thrown open to let in the morning sun. The harsh screech of seagulls served as counterpoint to mockingbird songs. Fine linen covered the table, and food was served on heavy silver platters. Dinnerware was delicate New Orleans porcelain edged in gold leaf; silver eating utensils were suitable for the table of a monarch.

Lafitte played the generous host. Reyna and Catherine waited at table. Father Francis offered a lengthy invocation.

Several times, the British captain tried to turn the discussion toward the war with the Americans. Deftly, Lafitte steered the conversation away from politics.

"No talk of business until our meal is complete," he insisted, making it clear that to do otherwise was a major breach of etiquette in Louisiana.

The three officers, obviously impressed by the pirates' hospitality, ate and ate and ate. After three or four hours at the dining table, Lafitte yielded to their obvious discomfort and led his guests and cohorts to the courtyard patio. A wide iron grilled gate allowed the slight sea breeze to stir the palmettos planted along the interior eight-foot wall. The noonday sun beat down relentlessly on the glazed brick floor. Cypress furniture was arranged for seating, but Jean chose to sit in the only hardback chair at the cypress log table.

The British Navy captain settled uncomfortably on the edge of the deep-seated cypress chair. Reyna hid her smile when he pulled a rough wood splinter out of the seat of his pants. "Ah," he said, "now to our business,"

"Oh, no, not yet," said Lafitte, who snapped his

71

fingers, and sent Reyna scurrying to fetch a silver tray holding six snifters and a crystal decanter of rare old brandy. Catherine returned with fine Cuban cigars.

Reyna watched the British in wool uniforms drown in their own sweat while Lafitte and his men lounged in lightweight cottons. She leaned against the courtyard wall behind Lafitte, in case she should be needed. Catherine disappeared into the house. A combination of sun, too much food, and wine mellowed the British officers so that they could hardly speak. Finally, Lafitte reached for the British packet of papers and laid them out on the table.

Several pages long, the first document was an appeal to Louisianians to join the English against the United States, signed by the commander of His Majesty's forces in the Floridas. Jean read aloud several flowery passages.

"Natives born to Louisiana!" he read. "On you, we make our first call. Assist us, please, in liberating your paternal soil from a faithless imbecile government."

The commander's letter described the might of the British forces, which included a large body of Indians. "These brave red men burn only with a desire to satisfy the wrongs they have suffered from Americans . . ." It ended, "I guarantee everything I have promised in this paper on my sacred honor as a British officer."

Jules, hardly able to contain his ridicule, paced the courtyard, ending up in front of Reyna. "Bring me some water, girl," he said. "I'm having a bit of trouble swallowing."

Reyna stole a look at the Englishmen, who did not comprehend his insult.

Lafitte was reading the second document when she returned with a pitcher of water. He smoothed the paper out and spoke. "His Majesty wishes the commandant of Barataria to join the British Navy, and promises rewards to me and my men.

"It says, 'You shall have the rank of captain . . . your property shall be guaranteed and protected . . . your ships will be placed under the commanding officer of this station . . . you may be a useful assistant in forwarding my proclamation to the inhabitants of Louisiana.'

"Listen to this," he read pointedly, " 'A powerful reinforcement is on its way here.' " Lafitte exchanged glances with Jules and Picou.

Reyna wondered if the British really did have reinforcements on the way, or were they bluffing?

The third letter consisted of orders given to the Navy commander who was now Lafitte's sated guest. "In the event the men of Barataria are not inclined to act offensively against the United States, you must do everything in your power to persuade them to a strict neutrality . . ."

Picou made a show of resting his hand on the pistol at his waistband.

The fourth letter, dated two days later, carried a more direct threat: "British merchantmen have been detained, taken, and sold by the inhabitants of Barataria; therefore, Captain Lockyer of His Majesty's sloop, *Sophia*, is to demand instant restitution. In case of refusal, I order him to destroy to his utmost every vessel there. He is to destroy the entire place . . ."

Lafitte drew a handkerchief from his pocket and wiped his mouth in a pretense of fear.

One of the Brits managed to pull himself up out of his low-slung chair, and said, "Lafitte, you will

73

be given thirty-thousand dollars and the rank of captain in the British Navy. You are a Frenchman," he said. "Now that England and France are friends, your place is with us. Your own brother languishes in a New Orleans jail, and there is a price on your head. It must be clear to you that the United States is your enemy."

"Look, Lafitte," the British army captain added, "it is our plan to free the slaves and arm them against the white people who resist our authority, just as we have armed the Indians who now make their way toward New Orleans from Alabama and Mississippi."

Reyna's stomach felt queasy. This was what Sister Augustine had been talking about. The British intend to win this war, at any cost.

"Your plan seems almost perfect," the pirate said. "Excuse me while I speak with my trusted officers." Jules and Picou followed Lafitte out of the courtyard. Reyna remained, hands folded in front of her, eyes cast downward.

Triumphant, the army captain banged his fist on the table. "I've won him over. I'm certain he will join us." The others agreed. They slowly came to their feet, and stood about for a while, beginning to look uneasy when Lafitte did not immediately return.

Suddenly, shouts of "Kill the spies!" floated over the courtyard walls. From the sound of it, the pirates had massed outside Lafitte's house and were demanding that the British officers be taken captive.

Several Baratarians barged through the iron gateway. They pushed the officers up against the wall and disarmed them. "Take the Brits to the guardhouse," one shouted. The officers struggled, but their efforts were easily overcome.

Reyna did not know what to do. She didn't know

if this was real, or a stage-managed drama for the benefit of the English. She was relieved when Lafitte returned and shouted at his men to desist.

"How could you violate my hospitality in such a fashion?" he roared. Picou and Jules, and several others, formed an escort to lead the visitors back to their boats.

"Before you go," Lafitte said, "I want you to know I will take this matter under most serious consideration. I will talk it over among my officers, and will let you know my decision soon."

The British trio seemed disconcerted because he had not given them an immediate favorable answer. But what choice did they have? Hot, sick to their stomachs from overindulgence, and bruised from rough treatment, they seemed relieved to bid farewell to Grand Terre.

Chapter 21

"This is a pretty picture." Lafitte and his friends settled into the cool living area of his house and sipped more brandy. "We either help defeat the Americans at New Orleans or be destroyed by the British Navy."

"I say let's swim out to their warship, sneak aboard, and kill them all," said Picou.

"Moments ago," Jules noted, "you were the one who said to join them."

"Quiet!" Lafitte demanded. "I must think."

Picou and Jules, muttering between themselves, left the room.

Catherine and Reyna had been standing at the top of the staircase. When they heard the men leave, Catherine wiggled a curved finger at Reyna. "Come with me," she said.

Reyna sank to the lowest stairstep and watched Catherine quietly approach Lafitte. She walked up behind him, pressed his head back against her chest and massaged his temples with firm, circular motions.

"It is my decision," he said. "Mine alone. My men will do as I say."

"Yes," she agreed.

"I am first a Louisianian, and second a Frenchman."

"Yes."

"I hold no respect for the English. Yet what they say is true. Pierre rots in jail. When the Americans catch me, and they will, we will both hang."

"No, Jean, no." Catherine made soothing noises. "It will not come to that."

Lafitte stood and wrapped his arms around Catherine, swaying with her as though he rocked a baby. Reyna turned her head, not wanting to spy upon such an intimate moment.

Lafitte paced the room as he put his thoughts into words. "That I would accept as truth their promises is ridiculous! Thirty thousand dollars is a good bit, but I am a wealthy man. The goods in my warehouses are worth more than five-hundred-thousand dollars."

As he reached the staircase, his dark eyes settled upon Reyna. Jean helped her stand. His finger lifted her chin. "Ah, my Spanish beauty. What do you think of all this?" He waved his hand to take in the room and, she supposed, all of his worldly concerns.

"May I speak?" she asked.

"Of course."

"You are a leader of men, Jean Lafitte. And it seems to me that you love this country where you have made your home. You are rooted here. Your ships, your treasures, your Catherine . . ." Reyna smiled. "I think your mind is already made up: You will fight on the American side. You only hesitate so that you can figure out how to reap the most advantages."

Lafitte laughed. "You are a bright girl. And you

are right. The British have offered me the opportunity to be a hero. Reyna, get my writing tablet, pen, and ink.''

The two girls watched Lafitte set pen to paper. The first letter was to a dear friend in New Orleans, a member of the state legislature. He signed it with a flourish and handed it to Catherine. Reyna read over Catherine's shoulder.

Lafitte defended his privateering. He told of the British offer, and he warned that reinforcements were on the way. His pleas on his brother's behalf were heart-rending. In the final paragraph, he said he would ask the British for fifteen days to give them an answer.

''Are you hoping the Americans will outwit the British and defeat them here on your doorstep?'' Reyna asked. ''They will applaud you for warning them. And, perhaps, they will release Pierre as a sign of their appreciation.''

''Hush,'' he said. A gentle smile took the edge off his words. ''I have another letter to write—one to the governor himself.''

Reyna laughed when she read Jean's words to Governor Claiborne.

He wrote, ''I am the stray sheep, wishing to return to the fold.''

How melodramatic!

''I tender my services to defend Louisiana. All I ask in return is for you to leave me and my people alone.''

So gallant!

''I will instantly leave this country to avoid any suspicion that I might have cooperated with the enemy.''

A grand gesture!

Lafitte sealed the two letters and placed them with all of the British documents into a leather packet.

"Reyna, change your clothes. Dress befitting one who calls upon the governor," he said. "I am sending you to New Orleans to deliver my warnings."

Chapter 22

Catherine helped Reyna select a dress for the trip to the mainland. They decided on a plain dark-green muslin gown, and hoped it would not show stains from a twelve-hour voyage through the swamps. Reyna packed one change of clothes.

She secured her hair away from her face with a pair of jeweled combs. Her only other accessory was the emerald pendant Jules had given her.

Catherine promised to wait until she was gone before she told Sister Augustine about Reyna's mission as a courier. Wisely, she crammed a second bundle into the boat that included mosquito netting, food, water, a lantern, and a light blanket. The girls kissed each other good-bye.

Reyna sat sedately in the center of the pirogue, her bags nestled at her feet. Jules stood behind her, skillfully managing the long pole that pushed them away from the bank and into the placid green water.

"How will Jean get the English captain to wait fifteen days?" she asked, caught up in the adventure.

"Oh, if I know Jean, he will flatter the man beyond reason."

"Yes." Her lips parted in a broad smile. "He does have a way with words, the same as you." She tossed a teasing glance over her shoulder and saw that Jules was smiling, too.

This was Reyna's first trip off Grand Terre since she had been taken captive six months before. And it was her first encounter with the dashing Jules, away from prying eyes. She was full of wonder at how quickly the adventure had developed. One moment she was serving food and drink to British officers, and the next she was entrusted with a packet of letters for the governor. Her heart fluttered with anticipation. If Lafitte was a hero, then perhaps she was a heroine. In a small way, the safety of Louisiana was also up to her.

Only a few hours of daylight remained when they pushed off from Grand Terre, which meant they would be traveling mostly by night. *Jules must know the bayous well if he can navigate them by feel rather than sight,* she decided.

Entranced by the bayou country, Reyna was surprised at how quickly Jules maneuvered them through the watery maze. They traveled through a green tunnel, the branches of trees on both sides of the bayou meeting above their heads. The late afternoon sunlight, filtering through leaves and moss, was diluted, a glimmer rather than a glare.

Strange roots poked up through the shallow waters near the shore. Cypress knees, Jules called them. And sometimes, the water itself was covered with floating green plants, a liquid forest they sliced through as easily as a knife through butter.

"Ohhh, look," she said, her voice hardly above a whisper. A bobcat posed at the water's edge. Jules shoved the pole at him, and the cat snarled.

"Not afraid of us, is he?" Jules said. "It's a humbling experience to ride these waters. Humans seem the least of the species, rather than the mightiest. Look over there."

Reyna saw two eyes and a long snout floating off to the left. An alligator—ten feet long, she guessed. It swished its powerful tail in a kind of salute, then sank below the water's surface.

Jules explained that bayou meant "sleeping waters," because there was no discernible current. "But do not be deceived," he said. "These waters are treacherous. The calm you feel here is misleading. You think you are in Eden . . ."

His words lulled her.

Suddenly Jules jiggled the pirogue and banged the pole against the side of the boat. Reyna screamed.

". . . but do not be deceived. The bayou can change in a moment. The wind howls. The water chops up and down. Haven't you noticed the odd twisted shapes of the trees around here? The winds did that. They can be vicious. And the wildlife? Black bear, wolves, bobcats, alligators, cottonmouth moccasins. Keep your hands inside the boat, my dear."

"Captain LeFevre, you're trying to scare me."

"No. Nature will do that all by itself. Wait until dark."

When the newness of the scenery wore off, Reyna began to stretch and shift in her small wedged-in place.

"Getting tired?" he asked.

She twisted first one way, then another. "I wish we could get out and walk around a bit."

"Need a privy?"

Reyna blushed. "That would be nice."

"We will stop shortly at a trapper's cabin. You will meet a true Cajun. Don't be surprised if you can't understand a word he says. When we get back in the pirogue, there will be no stopping until we reach New Orleans."

Chapter 23

Reyna and Jules ate thick slices of greasy bacon, a white mushy corn cereal called grits, hard biscuits, and the most delicious wild-berry jelly Reyna had ever tasted.

The trapper's cabin was dark and dismal, lit with homemade beeswax candles. The floor was dirt, the roof thatched with palmetto leaves. Traps and fishing equipment littered the yard, and threadbare clothes fluttered on a line strung between two scrubby oaks. Muskrat hides dried on a rack near the smokehouse.

The trapper's wife was a thin, leather-skinned woman, whose eyes always seemed to be darting toward her husband, seeking his approval. She accompanied Reyna to the privy, which was hidden in a dense thicket behind the house. The stench was so nauseating that Reyna had to hold her nose to keep from being sick. As soon as she could, she hurried back to the cabin, glad to resume her place in the pirogue.

"Come again," the old man shouted. Reyna waved to the trapper and his wife, then snuggled into the boat, the light blanket under and around her, protecting her. Her back rested against the built-in wooden seat.

Light from the sky was no longer visible. How suddenly her world had turned black!

Jules LeFevre poled the boat steadily, seeing every crook in advance, although the flickering lantern in the bow pierced the darkness only slightly and mostly attracted moths and insects.

"We're making good progress," Jules said. "We should be there by daylight."

Soon the swamp's inky darkness was broken only by crimson reflections from the eyes of creatures watching them from the shore. An occasional skittering ghost of blue swamp fire and the flickering of dancing fireflies created an eerie backdrop as they sliced through still waters.

"It's scary out here," Reyna said. "We're so alone. What if something happened to you? What would I do?"

"Don't worry, my love. Nothing is going to happen to me."

"I am truly at your mercy." Reyna's nervous laugh sounded false even to herself.

"Aye," he said. "I've been thinking about that."

"You're just trying to scare me."

"Jean isn't here, you know. Neither is your overly protective holy woman."

"Stop it," she said. "Please." Reyna was sorry she had flirted with him.

Jules patted the thin packet of letters strapped to his body inside his shirt. "I'm not sure you realize the importance of your mission, my dear."

"I'm just a courier. I'm sure Jean did not want to spare any of his fighting men for such a small task."

"Umph."

They skimmed through the waters at a fairly fast pace with Reyna safely snuggled into her blanket, even though overhead branches seemed to have long black fingers that reached out to grab her. Frogs croaked so loudly, she feared one might jump into the boat, and the lonely hoot of owls echoed through the deep woods. Spanish moss rustled malevolently above her.

Even so, she eventually fell asleep.

Chapter 24

New Orleans

Jules secured the dugout at a ramshackle pier near the levee in New Orleans, then helped Reyna out of the boat. She stretched and yawned, hand-brushing her hair and smoothing her rumpled dress.

"How do I look?" she asked.

He picked a tiny piece of leaf off her forehead. "You look ravishing, my dear."

He carried her valise in one hand, took her arm with the other, and they walked toward the center of town. They stopped at an outdoor cafe for coffee, and Reyna took the opportunity to freshen up.

"The packet is addressed to John Blanque, a legislator who is a friend of Jean's," Jules said, as he handed her the leather pouch. "My orders are for us to take the letters to him, then you will accompany Blanque to see the governor."

"Where will you be?"

"Oh, I dare not go with you beyond Blanque's door. I would probably be arrested. I will watch from a discreet distance. We need some kind of code, though, since I won't be able to hear what is actually being said."

He thought for a moment. "I know. Tie your hair back with my scarf. If everything goes well, keep it on. But if things go awry, unbind your hair. I will rescue you."

Reyna's hand fluttered out to touch his chest. "Do you think I will need to be rescued? Surely not?" Her statement ended as a question.

"Don't worry, my love. You will be among the elite of New Orleans. Maintain your dignity, and support Jean in every way. Tell them that you, and only you, can give him their answer. That should be enough to make them let you go."

Reyna was quiet as they walked the muddy streets. Blanque's home was a narrow two-story brick house with a gate of black wrought iron featuring the family crest. Jules grabbed the brass door knocker, in the shape of a lion's head, and pounded on the door, the noise shattering the still morning. It was seven o'clock, but the household seemed to be asleep.

A maid, dressed in a black dress with white apron, answered the door. Her hair was loosely tucked beneath a white starched bonnet, and her arms were crossed.

"What you be wantin' this early?" She scowled.

Jules started to speak, but Reyna stepped forward. "I am Reyna Maria Alvaron. I was kidnapped by the pirates of Barataria six months ago. I carry important papers to Representative Blanque from Jean Lafitte . . . papers that warn of an imminent invasion of New Orleans. Take me to your master. Immediately!" Reyna's voice rang with authority.

The maid stepped back and allowed her to enter. Reyna turned to Jules, extended her hand formally, and thanked him for safely escorting her through the bayous. He made a show of kissing her knuckles, and winked flirtatiously, then disappeared around the corner.

Reyna entered Blanque's lovely New Orleans home.

Thirty minutes later, a hastily-dressed paunchy and balding Representative Blanque solemnly took the pouch from Reyna and bade her sit down in the parlor. She couldn't help but study the room while he read and reread the four documents and the letter addressed to him. The letter to the governor was sealed with wax and bore the imprint of Jean Lafitte's ring.

The parlor was dark and stuffy, and Reyna yearned for fresh air and sunlight.

Reyna set aside a tray laden with tiny jelly-filled tarts and French coffee when Blanque finished reading. The man removed his wire-framed glasses, and tapped them against his nose. His forehead was creased with tiny pouches of flesh that thinned to a web of laugh lines at the outside corners of his dark-blue eyes.

She leaned toward him. "So you see, sir, it is imperative that we reach the governor with this information as soon as possible."

"Yes." He studied her with a critical eye. "Did you like living on Barataria?"

"I admire Jean Lafitte," she said. "He has treated me with the utmost courtesy. Sister Augustine, who came with me from Spain, has also been dealt with kindly."

Blanque raised his eyebrows but Reyna did not understand his expression. "Come along," he said. Once they were outside the front gate, she stopped and patted her hair. If Jules was watching, he would see that she still wore the white silk scarf.

⚮

Chapter 25

The Governor's Mansion was just that—a mansion—whose size and grandeur intimidated Reyna. She and Blanque were asked to wait in the parlor while a servant roused Governor Claiborne. But Blanque left her alone so he could search out a maid to serve them coffee.

Reyna fidgeted. Her assignment was to impress the governor with the danger of an immediate invasion and to win clemency for Jean and Pierre.

Blanque returned and handed her a silver tray, bearing beignets, French donuts, and a carafe filled with dark-roast coffee.

She set the tray on a marbletop table, preparing to serve Blanque, but he retreated from the room, and closed the heavy double doors behind him. An outside lock snapped into place.

Reyna willed herself to pour the coffee into a fragile porcelain cup and sip at it as she crossed the room and pulled aside a lace curtain. *I am trapped here, Jules. Are you out there? Are you watching? This is not the treatment I expected.*

Reyna waited for more than an hour. Men came

and went through the foyer outside her door. Air in the room seemed close. Fear made her claustrophobic. *I can't stand this,* she thought, *not a minute longer.*

She walked to the thick wooden doors and rapped several times. She knocked again more loudly. When it appeared she was being ignored, she beat on the doors with both fists.

"Let me out of here!" She continued to pound against the doors until she collapsed against them in tears.

Suddenly, they were thrown open and she stumbled into the hallway.

A woman, beautifully groomed and wearing a fine white-linen day gown, caught her arm as she fell forward. The woman's complexion was flawless and her large dark eyes were bright with intelligence. A thick mane of ebony hair slicked away from her face, accenting a pronounced widow's peak. Secured in a tight bun, the severity of the hairstyle only enhanced her heart-shaped face.

"My dear, what on earth is going on?" The aristocratic tilt of the Spanish woman's head made her seem to be looking down at Reyna, although she wasn't much taller than Reyna herself.

Reyna gasped for breath. "I've been locked in that room for hours. I could not breathe." She overdramatized. "How dare they treat me in such a fashion!"

"Come, come. I do not know what is going on here, but I will find out."

The woman, whom Reyna assumed to be the governor's wife, opened the drawing room doors with a flourish. "William, why have you locked this lovely young girl in the parlor?"

Six men, including Blanque, looked up. One man rose from his place at the head of the table and glided toward them. The others all stood in deference to the females.

"My dear, this is a meeting of the gravest importance." The man held himself tall and stiff, almost regal, yet he kissed the woman's cheek and extended his hand for Reyna's as he made a courtly bow. "I am William C. C. Claiborne, governor of Louisiana. And you are the emissary of the notorious Jean Lafitte?"

Reyna gathered her wits and spoke with all the authority she could muster. "I have come on Lafitte's behalf, and on the behalf of all the citizens of Southern Louisiana. Lafitte can help you turn the British away from your door. In good faith, he sent those documents to you. You must give him an answer straightaway."

"I hear your plea," the governor said. "The welfare of this state, as well as the entire country, may rest upon what we decide here today. I have called together several of my advisers, military and civilian." He indicated the men at the banquet table.

Claiborne, a dashing figure even in informal dress, took both women by their arms and gently led them out into the hallway. "My dear," he said to his wife, "would you see to the comfort of Senorita Alvaron while we continue our meeting?"

The woman's dark eyes flashed at her gray-pompadoured companion. "This young lady is a guest in our home, William. I will not abide her being locked in a room and disregarded in such a surly manner."

She turned to Reyna and nodded toward the staircase, speaking loud enough for her husband to over-hear. "In the olden days, they killed the messenger of bad tidings. I did not realize Louisiana had slipped so far back into the Dark Ages."

Chapter 26

Reyna was taken to a well-appointed bedroom at the front of the house. A maid brought hot water for her to bathe in. Another servant ironed her change of clothes and left it on the bed.

Impatiently, Reyna dressed and groomed herself. So far she had been ignored by the governor. When she was called downstairs, she wanted to be prepared, physically and mentally, to carry his message of approval back to Barataria.

No doubt he would want Jean's help in halting the wave of British soldiers. *How can the man want otherwise?*

Restless and nervous, she tried the door several times to be sure she had not been locked in. Even so, she believed herself to be more imprisoned here than she had ever been on Grand Terre.

French doors opened onto a narrow balcony enclosed with cast iron filigree. *The blacksmith who made the ironwork was an artist,* Reyna thought, as she considered the grapevine trellis of iron, painted a cool sea green. *Hadn't the Lafittes owned a blacksmith shop in New Orleans before they turned to lives of crime? Wouldn't it be a coincidence if this magnificent balcony had come from their smithy?*

Reyna forced her mind to concentrate on more important matters. For instance, there was no means of escape.

She paced in and out periodically, hoping Jules was nearby, would see her, and would note that she still wore the white scarf around her hair.

A maid came at lunchtime to take her to the courtyard where she was served an elegant shrimp salad ringed with tropical fruits. The courtyard, she noted, had a wide carriageway and one passageway that led out of the grounds. Lanterns hung on either side to light the night. A stairway led to slave quarters.

The courtyard was an intimate high-walled garden. Vines embraced the thick brick walls. Flowering plants in huge urns were placed strategically on the brick terrace, but sweet-smelling hedges, and palm and banana trees grew in a lush, wild manner around its edges.

As Reyna finished her meal, the governor's wife came outdoors to join her. Mrs. Claiborne made Reyna feel less of a hostage and more like a guest. Discreetly, the woman questioned Reyna about her past, her life with the pirates, and, especially, about Jean Lafitte. She also learned of the marriage contract to Don Carlos Vasquez.

The girl tried to answer the questions as directly as possible. She hoped she had found an ally.

"You know," Mrs. Claiborne said, "I believe I may have met your Monsieur Lafitte last year, although he was traveling under a different name. I was visiting a friend at her country home, and found the most delightful gentleman had come calling—a

Monsieur Clement. He was a fascinating individual, and very handsome.''

She went on to describe the man in detail. Reyna could not help but agree. It did sound like Jean.

''We shared a lovely meal and a congenial evening. Sparkling repartee, continuous laughter. I sensed my friend wished the evening to end, but I could not allow her to separate me from this charming man until quite late. The next day I returned to New Orleans, but I admit, I was enchanted with Monsieur Clement.''

Mrs. Claiborne's face lit up while she told her story. Reyna thought perhaps the governor's wife was still fascinated and intrigued by the handsome stranger.

The woman sighed. ''I am so protected here. I did glimpse a man in the square one day, who looked a great deal like Monsieur Clement. The man was identified to me as Jean Lafitte, the dashing privateer. I could never be absolutely certain it was the same man, but I suppose I would like to think so.''

''But your husband and Jean are enemies,'' Reyna said.

''I never allow politics to interfere with my social life,'' Mrs. Claiborne said.

Reyna hesitated. ''I am baffled by the way I have been treated by your husband. The safety of this city may depend on how quickly I get back to Barataria. Why is he taking so long to make a decision that is obvious even to me?''

''My child. Much goes on in Louisiana that is beneath the surface. Certainly William is concerned about the possibility of invasion. Likewise, he must please the military and civilian leaders who help him remain in office. I do not ask what goes on behind closed doors. Sometimes it is better not to know."

Asked to return to the guest room to wait, Reyna again paced between bed and balcony, hoping Jules would see that she still wore the white scarf. Finally, she collapsed onto the deep fluffy bed, which was dressed in starched white linens, and fell into an uneasy sleep. She woke at five o'clock, when a maid came to her door and summoned her to the drawing room.

John Blanque swiftly tucked his chin down and asked to be excused. She could not read his expression, but she thought he acted either embarrassed or ashamed. After much backslapping, the other men shook hands with the governor and left, too. Their moods seemed jovial and relaxed.

Reyna decided to be bold. "What is the message you wish me to take to Lafitte?"

"My dear," the governor began, "all of this is really none of your concern. But since you are somewhat involved, let me say that we have determined two things during our deliberations this afternoon. One, we do not believe these letters from the British are genuine. Two, we have determined it is not proper for me to hold any discussions with a wanted man, a thief and murderer as Lafitte surely is."

"But—"

The governor took Reyna's hands. "Surely you do not expect me to return a lovely and gentle lady such as yourself into the hands of so desperate an outlaw? It would be irresponsible of me. My wife has told me about the Spaniard, Don Carlos Vasquez. I will see to it that he receives a message regarding your well-being. You will remain in my house until he comes for you. The nun, Sister Augustine, will be the subject of a rescue mission by my militia. She will soon join you here."

"Are you saying you would keep me here against my will?" Reyna demanded.

The governor's voice was cold. "I am saying you will remain here under my protection. If you prefer to consider yourself a victim, we shall call it 'house arrest.' Dorrie . . ." He shouted for the maid. When she appeared at the door, he directed her to escort Reyna to her room.

Once in the foyer, Reyna made a dash for the front door. She got it halfway open before the hefty guard, who had been lingering outside the drawing room, grabbed her by the waist and hauled her toward the staircase.

"How dare you?" she sputtered. "Get your hands off me!" She beat her fists against his shoulder, but the guard lifted her off the floor.

"I'm sorry, miss," he said. "I have my orders."

She kicked his shin.

"You little . . ." He cursed.

He threw Reyna over his shoulder like a sack of potatoes and carried her, kicking and screaming, up the staircase, releasing her only when he got her inside the guest room. As he left, he dropped a latch over one of the outside knobs on the wooden double doors. Reyna was again a prisoner.

The girl did not hesitate one second. She walked resolutely to the French doors, threw them open, and stepped out onto the balcony. With a flourish, Reyna tore the white scarf from her hair and waved it back and forth, high above her head.

CRCR

Chapter 27

Within hours, Commodore Patterson of the United States Navy assembled forces for a two-pronged attack on the pirates. The man who would lead the U.S. troops through the bayous to Grand Terre was the exile, Garbeaux.

After dinner, Reyna watched from the balcony as the one-armed pirate swaggered out of the governor's mansion, clutching a leather purse that appeared to be heavy with coins. How she hated him!

The next morning, Dorrie, the maid, served her breakfast in bed, and told her someone had raided the New Orleans calaboose during the night and maneuvered the escape of Pierre Lafitte and three black men.

Reyna remained in her room until ten o'clock, when she was summoned to an audience with Governor Claiborne.

"My dear young lady." His voice was stern. "You have full reign of the house until this matter at Barataria is put to rest. Do not abuse your privileges."

Reyna tossed her head, and sniffed, as though she

smelled a foul odor. She deliberately turned away from him, vowing to use her captivity, in any way possible, to help the pirates. She would listen intently to everything and, as soon as possible, she would escape.

But what good would it do to escape when there was no chance of returning to Grand Terre anyway?

She had signaled that she needed help—the white scarf was now tied to the balcony railing. But no one had come. *Where is Jules? Doesn't he know I am a prisoner? Doesn't he care?* Reyna despaired.

The governor's wife tried to make Reyna comfortable by including her in the numerous social activities held at the mansion, but the girl always declined the invitations. The sturdy guardsman watched her every move while the servants were courteous but wary.

Reyna lapsed into depression. She could not even get excited about the beautiful gowns the governor's wife bought for her to wear during her incarceration. She was imprisoned, albeit in luxury, while Sister Augustine, Jean Lafitte, and Jules awaited her return, unsuspecting of the American military force being mounted against them, led in part by the traitor Garbeaux.

A fortnight later, she wondered if Jean was still hopeful of receiving a favorable response from the governor. Had the British given up their watch on the island? Had they become impatient with Lafitte's many excuses? Would they hoist anchor and sail away? Or would the enemy invade Barataria and come one giant step closer to New Orleans?

Chapter 28

September 16, 1814
Barataria

Lookouts spotted a fleet of warships entering the Gulf passage between Grand Terre and Grand Isle one bright September morning. Church bells pealed warnings even before the ships could be identified.

Sister Augustine watched from a vantage point near the chapel and wondered if, from above, Grand Terre looked like an anthill—the way the pirates rushed to and fro preparing defenses.

Father Francis grasped her by the arm and swung her around to face him, his expression one of deep concern. "The chapel is not safe," he said. "Our cross stands higher than the trees and makes an excellent target. Go to Lafitte's house and stay with Catherine. Make a bunker there for the women and children."

"Are the British returning?" Sister Augustine, normally spunky and decisive, had become a tired, old woman when she learned the Louisiana governor was holding Reyna captive.

The priest ignored her question. His first concern was to protect the sacrament in the tabernacle. Then he gathered every candlestick and chalice he could find, and piled them into a sack he could barely lift.

"Take these, Sister. Get someone to help you. Set up a field hospital, gather supplies. Do whatever you deem necessary to safeguard the defenseless. I will be with Jean."

Sister held fast to his arm. "Father, it is you who should assume leadership of the island."

"No, my place is with Lafitte. You take charge of the women and children. Now go! Hurry! The assault has already begun."

True enough, cannon shells exploded as she made her way through the horde of pirates running toward the beach.

Then someone screamed, "It ain't the Brits! It's the Americans!"

Sister, shading her eyes, focused on the American flag fluttering from the bow of the lead vessel. The pirates almost trampled her when they left their posts and began to scatter. So strong was sympathy for the United States, it appeared not one man wished to fire on American ships.

Sister hastened to Lafitte's house, calling to the women and children who stood around, confused and abandoned. Where was Lafitte? Catherine? Picou? Jules? Why were the Americans firing on the island?

No matter. She must do what Father ordered. She shouted over the din of gunfire as she organized teams. Several women and children were sent to gather food, firewood, and water. The strongest and heftiest youths, none older than twelve, helped shove large pieces of furniture in front of doors and windows, effectively barricading the inside of the house.

Smoke filtered in from the cannonade, as did the sharp pungent odor of gunpowder. Grapeshot bounced against the outer walls.

How strange it seemed to be hiding from Americans, when they were the people Lafitte wanted to help!

Huddled in the lower quarters of Lafitte's house, Sister Augustine managed to feed and care for a group of thirty women and twenty children. She robbed the upstairs of all the bedding, and set it up in the center of the room. The thick banquet table and the cypress table from the courtyard were placed on their sides as a wedge of extra protection.

As darkness approached, Sister wondered if the invaders felt they had earned a rest. Had they killed their quota? Gunfire ceased, replaced by a quiet that seemed more deafening than the constant barrage.

The women remained silent as they prepared a simple meal. Sister lit one candle, and placed it on the staircase so people could find their way to the chamber pots under the stairs.

Sister Augustine's apathy after the loss of Reyna was replaced by a fierce determination. She'd been asked to protect these people, and, with God's help, she would do so!

The second day began with sporadic shooting at dawn. As the sun rose, so did the level of noise. The day continued much like the first, except more screams and curses seeped in from under the thick doors.

Stationed near the main door, the nun was peeking through a window grille when, suddenly, a screaming woman jumped on her and hit her, delivering a fast and fierce beating so quickly that everyone was caught off guard.

"My husband's out there! Let him in!" The woman screeched and flailed at Sister Augustine with both fists.

"I can't. I can't." The nun covered her face, fearing the woman would scratch out her eyes. The older boys tore the frantic woman off and pinned her arms behind her. "I cannot allow a breach of our defenses, no matter who is outside," Sister said. "Please understand."

Blood trickled from a cut near Sister's left eye, and a swelling blue bruise was forming on her cheekbone. She feared her legs would fold beneath her, but she managed to remain standing, to remain in control.

The woman collapsed in a faraway corner. Children bawled.

The household became disheartened, without hope.

Nighttime again brought a silence so dense it was palpable. Firelight flickered outside where homes had been torched. Bodies were scattered on the ground, unmoving.

"Dear God," Sister whispered, "take care of the Lafitte brothers. They do not deserve such treachery from those whom they were trying to help."

For two days, the women and children made do with the food at hand. Most of the time, they spoke in whispers, if they spoke at all, always straining to hear what was going on outside.

The morning of the third day, a man pounded on the main door and demanded, "Open up. We know you're holed up in there and, if you don't allow us entry, we will torch the place." A whoof of air escaped from Sister, sounding as if she'd been hit in the stomach.

Everyone looked to the nun to do something. She crossed herself, then shouted back, "I am Sister Augustine. I have defenseless women and children in here. What will become of us, if I let you in?"

The man's voice seemed slightly more respectful. "You will not be harmed. Women and children will be taken to New Orleans and set up in camps, dispersed at their choosing to live on plantations or remain in the city. We are anticipating an invasion by the British. We need all the help we can get."

"What of the men?" she asked.

He hesitated. "We have some eighty in custody. Many are wounded. A fair number have died. Most, however, have escaped into the marshes. And that includes the Lafittes. Open up, in the name of the United States government."

Sister Augustine studied the faces of those gathered around. She hunched her shoulders. *What else can I do?* She ordered, "All of you, get behind the tables and do not show yourselves until I say so."

When everyone was hidden, two boys helped her push the sideboard away from the front door. As soon as the boys were back in place, Sister unlatched the bolt and slowly opened the door.

A half-dozen American soldiers, with guns drawn, rushed into the house and took up posts around the room. The army captain acknowledged Sister with a curt nod. He peered over the banquet table, and began to count people.

"Please rise, all of you. Walk outside, single file. Identify yourselves and give the names of your menfolk. When possible, we will tell you their circumstances. We will take you to New Orleans by ship. Again, I say, if you behave, you will be treated fairly."

Chapter 29

October 1814
New Orleans, The Governor's Mansion

"Reyna, I have good news for you," the governor said at the dinner table one night. "Your
rich Spanish landowner, Don Carlos Vasquez, has
sent word he will arrive within a few weeks to take
possession of you."

Blood crept up to flush her face, and the governor
laughed at her expression. "No, child, I do not wish
to be rid of you, as I assume you think. It will be to
your benefit to be gone from New Orleans before the
battle begins, for there will be a battle. The British
lurk outside our portals, constantly adding to their
forces. They will be here before we know it."

"What of you and Mrs. Claiborne?" asked Reyna,
ignoring her own precarious future.

"I will die in the defense of this city." He was
unable to conceal his bitterness. "I have pled with
the government to send me troops. I have written
countless letters to the governors of Tennessee and

Kentucky, begging for volunteers. Yet no help comes.''

He bowed his head and held empty hands out in front of him, as if the heavy weight of saving the Crescent City rested entirely in the palms of his hands. He raised his eyes to meet Reyna's, then lingeringly focused on every feature of his wife's loving face.

Reyna knew Mrs. Claiborne was already packed for a retreat upcountry. She would leave at the first sign of an emergency. Even though she balked at the idea, her husband had ordered her to be ready.

''Governor, what if I do not like Don Carlos? What if I do not wish to marry him?''

Mrs. Claiborne smothered a smile with an upraised hand, after registering the shock on her husband's face. ''My dear,'' she said, ''you intended to marry the man only a few months ago. You left the convent, crossed an ocean. You had no qualms then. Why now?''

''I'm not the same person who left the convent in Spain. I've grown up.'' Reyna shrugged. She didn't understand, either, all the changes that had taken place inside of her.

''Ah, I see,'' the lady said. ''And you've been charmed by the handsome pirate Jean Lafitte, too, I gather?''

Reyna knew the significance of the word ''too.'' The women exchanged a knowing glance.

''But what if . . .?''

''Never you mind,'' the governor's wife said. ''I'm sure you will be just as bewitched by this Spaniard as you have been by these reckless privateers. Mark my word. You will come to adore the man, in time.'' She glanced toward her husband and smiled.

Reyna toyed with her food. "Have you news of Sister Augustine and the others?"

"They should arrive any day. You will be reunited with your Spanish nun before you leave for Tejas," he said.

Later, Reyna, wearing a gown the same shade as the flame-colored hibiscus that bloomed on her balcony, stood in shimmering moonlight and leaned against the iron railing, considering her lack of options.

If only Jules or Jean or Picou would come to her rescue. If only Sister Augustine would arrive in time to stop this marriage. If only she had more control over her own life.

I am tired, she thought, *of being a pawn in the hands of strangers.*

Chapter 30

A t midnight, horses were reined in at the front of
the Governor's Mansion, and someone banged
heavily on the door. Reyna was startled awake. Who
could be arriving so late?

Gently, she pushed open the French doors, and slid
to her knees so she would not be seen from below.
She edged to the railing and looked over. Several
men in uniform spoke urgently with the butler and
were admitted to the entry hall.

Reyna considered slipping out to the staircase to
eavesdrop, but should she? She decided she should,
and was gathering her nightdress to stand up when a
wagon bumped along the rutted street and stopped
below.

Immediately, she recognized the passenger. "Sister
Augustine," she cried, leaning out over the railing.

"Reyna, my child, thank God you are unharmed."
Sister started to rise, intending to dismount, but the
butler suddenly ordered the driver to take the wagon
to the back entrance. The driver yelled "Giddiup"
and Sister was dumped back onto the wooden seat.

Servants lit lanterns throughout the courtyard as

the governor and his wife bustled outside in their robes.

Mrs. Claiborne took Sister's arm and graciously led her toward the house. "How tired you must be from your journey, and hungry, too, I imagine. I will have the maid bring up a tray and prepare a bath for you. You'll be in the bedroom adjoining Reyna's."

"Thank you," murmured Sister. Her arm rested on Reyna's shoulders, and together they followed the governor's wife upstairs.

Behind a hastily set up screen, Sister Augustine bathed quickly in the warm water brought by the servants, and readied herself for a much-needed rest in the welcoming feather bed. Perched at its foot, Reyna waited for the nun to complete her ablutions. When Sister emerged in her nightdress, not only had she washed away the road dirt but her fears as well, or so it seemed to Reyna.

After formal prayers, Reyna lay down next to Sister, their hands tightly clasped together.

"Sleep here," Sister said quietly. "I want to know that you are near."

"I won't leave you," said Reyna, "not ever . . ." She paused, then completed her thought. "And you won't ever leave me, will you?"

Sister Augustine didn't answer. She had already slipped into peaceful slumber.

Chapter 31

Several days later, Reyna and Sister Augustine sat in the courtyard, enjoying a brief sunny respite after a weekend of slow drizzle. A carriage pulled into the drive and two men emerged.

Both removed their hats in the presence of the women.

The older man, who had to be at least thirty, wore a thin mustache, and leaned heavily on a cane. His face was leathery and his dark eyes stared out over the eagle beak of his nose. He spoke first. "I am Carlos Xavier Vasquez from Tejas. I have come for my betrothed."

Sister Augustine stepped forward, shielding Reyna from the men.

"I am Sister Augustine from the orphanage in San Leandro. I accompanied Reyna here. She is in my charge and I shall not release her until I am certain of your intentions."

Don Carlos glanced at his companion and raised his eyebrows. "Feisty old nun, isn't she?"

Reyna was appalled by his disrespect. *Surely he isn't that crude!*

The Spaniard clicked his heels together and made an exaggerated bow. "My intentions were good enough when I offered a generous donation to your orphanage."

Sister's steely eyes bored into the man. She folded her arms across her chest and glowered.

There was an uneasy silence.

Don Carlos stepped forward as if to go around Sister. "Is this lovely lady . . . ?"

Reyna self-consciously patted the dark curls that cascaded around her shoulders, then stepped out to greet him. "I am Reyna," she said, and curtsied both to Don Carlos and to the younger man at his side.

Benito Sandoval removed his hat and clicked his heels, imitating Don Carlos.

"Forgive my manners," Don Carlos said in a stilted manner. "I've been on the road too long. This is my second-in-command, Benito Cruz Sandoval."

The younger man flashed a smile. Sister wrung her hands and scowled.

Don Carlos attempted to win approval. "Last spring, I sent Benito down here for more than a month to search these blasted swamps for the two of you. Only a bullet wound kept him from completing his mission."

The younger man's gaze probed Reyna.

Are all men from Tejas brutes? Pirates have better manners than these two.

Benito Sandoval was slightly shorter than Don Carlos, and his skin was a richer, darker brown. His hair, straight and black, hung unkempt to his shoulders.

The governor bustled outside and gripped Don Carlos's hand in a hearty handshake, urging him toward the house for a tot of whisky. Benito was included in the invitation, but he elected to remain outside with the carriage and their gear.

"Please be seated," Reyna said, graciously acting the hostess. She indicated a wicker chair across from hers. "Was your journey long and tedious?"

"Not so bad," Benito answered. "Part by boat, part by horseback. We were stopped at several roadblocks leading into the city. It appears New Orleans is preparing for war."

"God forbid it come to that," Sister said, making the sign of the cross. The two young people automatically copied her, then smiled at each other to be caught in identical involuntary movements, rising out of the rigorous religious training they both had received in their youth.

Suddenly Reyna couldn't stop fidgeting. This man was staring at her so . . . so ferociously. Finally she gripped her hands in front of her to still them, and felt herself blush.

"Did you come to Barataria looking for me?" she asked.

Benito nodded. "That was an ill-fated day," he said. "All I learned was that you were still alive. I was almost trampled to death by this huge bald pirate, and then I was shot and chased through the swamps back to my boat. I barely escaped."

Sister and Reyna exchanged glances. Somehow Reyna was pleased he had not boasted about Tomas's death.

"You killed a man," she said, "a friend of mine. Tomas . . . he was a good man. He cared about me . . . he . . ."

Distressed, Benito spoke in a rush of words. "Please, Senorita, I only fought with him in self-defense. The gun went off as we struggled. I did not intend to kill him.''

Reyna studied his dark sensitive eyes and could see no gloating, no sparkle of pride.

There was an uncomfortable silence until Sister Augustine spoke. "Tell me, sir, about The Anchorage, about life in Tejas. Set my mind at ease that Reyna will be treated with kindness, and will be well taken care of, since I will not be accompanying her.''

"What?" Reyna sank to her knees in front of the nun. "This is the first I've heard of your not coming with me. What are you thinking? Where will you go?''

Benito stepped backward, as if to separate himself from their conflict.

"I decided weeks ago," the nun said. "During the raid on Grand Terre. I have found my place of service with the women and children of Barataria. And the Bishop agrees. I have a mission here, dear Reyna. You no longer need me. You will fare well, wherever you are. Just look at how you've been accepted here in the house of a governor.'' Sister took a deep breath. "Child, how can I flee to safety when others so desperately need me?''

Reyna did not try to hide the tears that glistened on her cheeks. She placed her head on Sister's lap, as she had done during the voyage from Spain. "I feel so alone," she said. "After all that's happened, it never occurred to me that you wouldn't come with me. I never thought you'd forsake me to these . . . to these strangers.'' She motioned toward Benito.

The young man bowed slightly. "I am sorry to intrude, but it was never Don Carlos's intent that the nun accompany you to Tejas. I was given a purse full of coins to pay for her passage back to Spain.''

Reyna and Sister Augustine's startled looks quickly brought about his leave-taking. "This is a personal discussion between you. Please excuse me while I look for Don Carlos. We still must find an inn."

While he spoke, his eyes never left Reyna. She felt a twinge of curiosity, but more important things needed her attention at the moment. Sister Augustine planned to abandon her.

Reyna fled to her room and threw herself onto the bed, anticipating a long jag of crying, but surprised herself when her tears were short-lived. She rolled onto her back and stared at the twelve-foot ceiling. The last time she gave in to musings about Tejas, her ship was overtaken by pirates and her life changed irreversibly. *Here I am, at another crossroads,* she thought. *How will I manage? How can I go on— alone?*

For dinner that evening, Reyna dressed formally in one of the gowns purchased for her by Mrs. Claiborne. It was rose-colored satin, overlaid with silver-tipped lace. The dress clung to her form, yet the lace covered her from the gown's high neck to fingertip points at her wrists.

Her raven hair was piled on top of her head, and Jules's emerald pendant lay at the crevice of her bosom.

Don Carlos stared hungrily at Reyna all evening, so much so that she shivered in unconcealed discomfort. Benito seemed to fade into the background when his captain was near, yet she remained always aware of his presence.

"My land is *muy magnifica.*" Don Carlos waved his hands expressively in the air. "The plains stretch as far as the eye can see. The sky is usually a pristine blue, dotted by clouds of purest white. The sun can be merciless, but adobe keeps our houses cool. Winters are mild.''

Don Carlos dominated the dinner table with his word portraits, describing celebrations that lasted for days and bragging of his wealth and prestige.

"What about your religious life?'' asked Sister. "You have not mentioned a priest to officiate at the wedding.''

"Do not worry.'' Don Carlos waved his hand in dismissal. "We can be married here before we leave or I'll send for a priest. Did I mention that I intend to build a chapel on the grounds so that my beautiful Reyna will have her own place to worship?''

The more wine he drank, the more expansive he became.

Repulsed by Don Carlos's attempts to impress her, Reyna remained quiet. And for some odd reason, she kept sneaking peeks at Benito, who, though silent, seemed more vibrant than Don Carlos.

When their glances met, Reyna swiftly turned away, angered by the stir she felt inside.

How can I possibly turn to this hired hand for help? He has no power against Don Carlos. What on earth is the matter with me?

⌒⌒⌒
Chapter 32

Reyna felt betrayed. She didn't exactly pout, but for several days she avoided Sister Augustine, who seemed to stay busy enough without her. Sister was always bustling through the house, directing the servants or taking extended trips into the swamps to visit Barataria refugees.

Reyna heard from Mrs. Claiborne that Sister had met the bishop, and had even called on the French nuns at the Ursuline Convent, seeking help for the swamp people.

What did it matter? Reyna was doomed to marry Don Carlos. He came to dinner every night, after spending a leisurely day in the coffee shops boasting, trading, and talking of war. Benito seldom came with him. Reyna wondered why.

At the dinner table, the Don continued his bragging, retelling his adventures for what seemed like hours. Finally, he would rise and ask Reyna to join him in the courtyard while he had a cordial.

She felt obligated to go, but in thirty minutes' time, she was gritting her teeth in irritation. Mrs. Claiborne and Sister Augustine saw to it that the couple was never left alone, a fact that did not escape Reyna's thankful notice.

She yearned for someone else to join them—even the mestizo or the governor—but this was Don Carlos's courting dance, and no one would intentionally break with tradition. So nightly, she suffered a constant barrage intended to impress her. Every evening he brought a new gift—a silver comb for her hair, a lace mantilla, an ivory fan.

He recounted his many adventures on the high seas, including how he saved Benito from a life of poverty and prison. He bragged about his money, his lands, and the vast inheritance of his father's wealth yet to come. He strutted for her, assuring her that he was much admired by women, suggesting that he was considered a good catch back in Tejas.

Reyna endured his braggadocio. But upon his departure each night, she fled to her room and cried herself to sleep. One midnight, she again tied the white scarf to the balcony railing in hopes Jules would venture by and understand that she was in distress.

She didn't want to leave with Don Carlos—not ever! Nor could she remain a guest in the governor's home forever. Neither did she want to go back to Spain. And Lafitte's community at Barataria had been destroyed. What were her options?

One Sunday afternoon, Don Carlos arrived unannounced and demanded that Reyna be awakened from her afternoon siesta, and be summoned to the parlor. When she entered, his back was turned and he leaned heavily on his cane. He seemed older than his professed thirty years.

She cleared her throat to announce her presence.

"Sit down," he ordered, his face a mask.

What emotion does it hide? she wondered.

Reyna placed herself in the center of the velvet loveseat, and spread her skirt around her, hoping to discourage the man from seating himself next to her. *Had something changed in their relationship?* Before he even opened his mouth, she knew he no longer courted her favors.

Don Carlos remained standing. His eyes narrowed to a squint, and he stomped his cane twice against the wooden floor. "I have waited long enough," he said. "I am needed back home. Furthermore, I have no wish to be sucked into a stupid war that offers me no benefits. Senorita, I am too old to play cat and mouse with you."

Reyna felt dominated by his presence. She started to rise.

"No, no, do not interrupt!" he said, holding his hand, palm outward, as if to physically stop her.

She sank back onto the settee.

"When I paid a full purse to the orphanage in Spain, I expected to receive a bride forthwith—a pure young woman to bear my children, a woman of grace and beauty who would comfort me in my old age. I grow older every day with this foolish courtship charade. Tell me, girl, why should I court you? You are bought and paid for."

He rolled his eyes in a show of exasperation but seemed to make a concerted effort to hold his temper.

"Reyna, don't you understand? There's a war brewing here. Thousands of British soldiers are on their way. It is doubtful Louisiana will continue to be American soil. Most women find me attractive. I have considerable wealth. And this leg does not keep me from doing anything. Anything!" he repeated.

He waved his hand at the room. "This mansion is a dung heap compared to what I can give you in Tejas. Girl, why do you even hesitate? You are mine, and I will not fall on my knees before you. Not you, or any woman!"

He stomped his cane to emphasize his words. "Tomorrow morning, be packed and ready. You know me well enough by now. When we get home, you can plan the most elaborate wedding ever seen. And until we are wed, you will remain as virtuous as you are at this very moment."

He glowered at her and Reyna wondered if he was being sarcastic. Was her virtue in doubt?

"May I speak, Don Carlos?" she asked respectfully.

"Make it brief." He paced the room.

"Sir, please understand that I am not the same girl who left Spain six months ago. I've been kidnapped by pirates. My life has been threatened, my shoulder dislocated by the same scum the governor uses to betray my friends.

"I am under house arrest in the home of the governor of Louisiana. Sister Augustine, who has been like a mother to me most of my life, may now be lost to me. And you want to rip me away from civilization, and have me become a servant to you, or worse, a figurehead of a wife, on some isolated frontier out in the middle of nowhere."

She paused, breathless. "I'm having doubts. Can't you understand that? I'm having doubts."

"Doubts, humph! I own you, girl. My money brought you here, otherwise you'd be rotting away in that convent." Don Carlos sneered as he bent toward her, his nose just inches from her face. "Doubts, you say? I'm the one who should be having doubts. You have lived a rather questionable existence these past few months. Perhaps you are no longer the innocent I require. Perhaps you are as worldly as the *bandidos* you've taken up with."

Don Carlos shook Reyna's shoulder roughly and snarled. "I may be your best chance to marry well. I may be your only choice."

He regained his height and dominion.

"You'll grow to like me, girl. You'll be a bright spot on the otherwise dull plains." Don Carlos stepped back. "You are dismissed. Go to your room and ready your belongings. We leave early tomorrow morning."

Reyna rose regally from the couch and preceded Don Carlos to the door. When she turned, her eyes brimmed with tears, her chin quivered, and her hand trembled on the doorknob. A deep well of anger boiled inside her. Her situation was hopeless, and she was helpless to do anything about it.

If I could, I'd slap him, the self-important bully! But what he says is true. What shall I do? She breathed deeply to smother the flames of fury that raged inside her.

Then Reyna surprised Don Carlos and herself. She faced him head-on.

"I shall go to my room . . . to consider my options. You, sir, do not own me—the donation you made was a gift, not a payment! I resent your challenge regarding my chastity. I *shall* decide my own fate, Don Carlos. And I will let you know my decision tomorrow."

∽∽∽

Chapter 33

Reyna had no one to turn to but God.

She spent the rest of the afternoon on her knees in prayer, begging for a miracle. She'd accept any kind of intervention—Jules, the governor, the war itself.

When she heard Sister Augustine return and prepare for bed, she did not go to the connecting doorway. She did not call out to her friend.

In the middle of the night, Reyna awoke to find herself, fully dressed, on the floor near her bed. Sleep had overtaken her during the grim search of her soul.

She pulled a valise out from under the bed and placed inside it the same dresses she had brought with her from Barataria. At her dressing table, she wrote a brief note, which she propped on her pillow. She swirled a green velvet cloak around her shoulders, and fastened it at the neck, patting her pocket to be sure she still had Jules's emerald. Then she surveyed the room one last time.

Headed down the staircase on tiptoe, Reyna crept past the maid's room, and unlatched the catch on the patio door. Her heart thumped wildly in her chest.

The tiny noise made by the latch seemed terribly loud in her current state of agitation. When the house remained silent, she pushed open the door and stepped out into the courtyard.

Her staccato footsteps clicked along the wet brick as she hurried to the carriageway. Reyna looked left and right, turned the corner, and was swallowed up by the dark, damp New Orleans night.

Chapter 34

Reyna knew she shouldn't go to the wharves after dark. She knew dangerous and violent people were about on the streets of New Orleans. Yes, and she knew that nice girls never appeared in public without an escort—and especially not in a city preparing for war.

But where else could she go? She had to escape Don Carlos. If only she had paid more attention when Catherine talked about her mother's house on the outskirts of the city. If only she could find someone on the wharves to direct her to Jean Lafitte's hiding place . . . if only it weren't so dark outside.

When a wagon approached, she slipped into the shadows and hid until it passed. She didn't want her presence to be noted. She didn't want to leave a trail for Don Carlos to follow.

As she pressed her body against the rain-slick brick, she could feel her heart pounding, and a terrible pain stabbed at the back of her neck. The dampness seeped through her cloak.

Jagged slices of lightning ripped through the black velvet sky while, nearby, thunder growled like a menacing mongrel. What a night to run away! But she'd had no choice! On the morrow, Don Carlos intended to drag her off to Tejas.

How angry would he be when he found her missing? Would Sister worry? Would the governor send guards to find her?

Reyna slipped from shadow to shadow, avoiding the brightly lit taverns and coffeehouses. When she reached the dock area, she burrowed into her cloak, its hood covering her dark hair and shielding her face. She found only one possible source of information.

A nattily dressed man of middle age walked thirty yards ahead. He whistled an off-key melody and performed a shuffle-kick dance every few paces. Had he just left a party? Was he happy or drunk? Reyna knew she was naive and might be exposing herself to harm, but to whom else could she turn?

"Sir, oh, sir," she called, hurrying toward him. He staggered slightly as he wheeled around.

"Please, senor, can you help me? I need to find someone right away—a friend—Jean Lafitte, the privateer. Perhaps you know him?"

The man swooped his hat toward the ground in an exaggerated bow. His smile seemed genuine enough but his eyes were wild and darting. She reeled from the smell of alcohol on his breath.

"I'll be your friend," he said, weaving menacingly toward her.

"No, no, it's all right. I've made a mistake. Excuse me, please." Reyna ran toward a dark area on the wharf where she could crouch behind huge bales of cotton awaiting transport.

"Where are you, girl? Don't run from me. I won't hurt you."

The tiny sips of breath she took through her mouth made her feel light-headed. Her cloak caught on a discarded piece of lumber, and held her captive. She crouched in the shadows.

"I'll be your friend." He begged pathetically while rain peppered down, accented by drumming thunder and brief brilliant flashes of lightning. He was only a few yards away, and she knew she was well hidden, but to Reyna, it looked as though he was staring right at her.

She did not speak, did not move. *Dear God . . .* she prayed.

Finally the man brushed the rain off his shoulders, and gave a little jig before returning to his midnight stroll. Relieved, Reyna gasped for breath, then spewed it out like air forced from a bellows.

Where can I go? She pulled frantically at her cloak until she heard it rip. *I am not crazy,* she told herself. *But hiding out here on the wharves in the middle of a stormy night is just that—crazy! What is wrong with me?*

Reyna inched from behind the cotton bales and scurried through the downpour toward friendly city lights, her valise bumping against her leg as she rushed along.

She stopped to catch her breath beneath the umbrella of an old oak tree and watched several men descend the outside stairs of a nearby coffeehouse. Their voices were raised in an argument about the war. Reyna recognized one of them—Representative Blanque, who had betrayed Jean Lafitte. She could not, would not go to him; he might betray her, too. Of course he might shelter her for the rest of the night. *But no,* she told herself. *Wait!*

A bowed elderly Negro waiter cleaned tables in

the open air cafe on the ground floor. Reyna stepped out of the shadows, wet, cold, and hungry.

Skittish as a colt, she moved toward the bent old man, ready to take flight at any sign of danger.

He spoke first. "Missy?" An unasked question lingered in his watery eyes.

Reyna risked her freedom on the compassion she saw written in the old man's face. She produced several coins from a small purse anchored to the waistband of her gown, and placed them on the round cafe table.

"I'll have coffee and a croissant, please." Her voice sounded brittle to her own ears, but she pretended nothing was out of the ordinary for a lone young woman to order food at midnight in a public coffeehouse.

The waiter returned with a steaming mug that he set in front of her. She inhaled deeply of the strong aroma, allowing it to revive her.

A few minutes later he ambled back with two croissants, butter, and honey. The man leaned forward as he refilled her cup and asked in a whisper, "You got troubles, Missy?"

Reyna nodded, deciding to confide in him. "I need a safe place to rest tonight. Somehow I must reach my friend—the pirate—Jean Lafitte."

His faded eyes grew wide at the mention of the notorious outlaw, but he said nothing, just turned and shuffled away. A lump formed in Reyna's throat. What did he think? What would he do?

When he returned, he bent toward her and whispered, "I know a place where you can go. Done sent a boy on ahead so they'll be expecting you. My son will carry your bag and lead the way, whenever you're ready, ma'am."

With a nod, he indicated a middle-aged Negro, dressed in a homemade uniform, lounging near the hitching posts.

Reyna hurried with her food. When she stood, the soldier walked over and picked up her bag.

"Where are you taking me?" she asked.

"We going to Madame Poreau's in the Quarter. Please follow close behind." His voice was a deep, reassuring bass.

The rain slackened and the thunder diminished to a muted rumble. Lightning blazed occasionally from the horizon on the other side of the Mississippi.

The soldier took the lead, while Reyna matched each of his long strides with two or three steps of her own.

Chapter 35

Madame Poreau's

Reyna was met at the back door of a two-story white-washed brick house that seemed to glow in the dark of the French Quarter. The black maid wore a navy blue robe over a long nubby cream-colored nightdress.

"Shh!" The maid shushed both Reyna and the soldier. "Our house is asleep. The missus say to take you upstairs and put you to bed right away." With a finger pointed at the door, the woman dismissed the soldier.

Reyna thanked the man with a weak smile, then followed behind the house servant, thoroughly intimidated. *I'll face the consequences tomorrow,* she thought, *after I've had a good night's sleep.*

"Water's in the basin, and a cloth. First door to the right at the top of the stairs. Sleeping clothes laid out on the bed. I'm wondering why you out this late, but the missus say don't ask no nosy questions. Just put you to bed, she say," the maid grumbled crossly.

Reyna hung her head, ashamed to have run away,

and sorry she had not had the confidence to face Don Carlos. *I hope Madame Poreau understands the desperation that drove me out into the night.*

Daybreak, the next morning

Benito sat in the driver's seat, the reins loose in his hands. Softly he whispered nonsense to quiet the horses while Don Carlos impatiently paced the courtyard.

"I don't understand why her bags aren't downstairs. She should have been dressed and packed and waiting for me."

Secretly glad Reyna was keeping his friend waiting, Benito laughed to himself. After all, they had arrived an hour before they were expected. The girl wasn't at all the stuck-up princess he had visioned. In fact, he found her to be soft-spoken and beautiful and intelligent and ... too good to waste away on the hot Tejas range. He wondered if he could stand being near her all the time, loving her, and she the wife of his best friend.

Loving her?

Impatient, Don Carlos pounded on the French doors.

Lights slowly came on throughout the house, and servants bustled about to prepare coffee and breakfast. A disheveled Governor Claiborne appeared in his nightshirt. "I looked for her," he said. "The girl isn't in her room. She left a note on her pillow. Here. It's addressed to you." He handed the piece of paper to Don Carlos.

Sister Augustine shrugged into a robe and clutched her nightgown closed at the neck as she hurried down the staircase, her concern for Reyna bleaching her face a deathly white.

Don Carlos read the note. With a look of utter disgust, he crumpled it into a wad and threw it into a puddle of the previous night's rainwater. His face turned red and his hands doubled into fists. Benito watched his friend's rage build. At the same time, his own heart thundered with fear for Reyna's safety.

"How dare she?" Don Carlos was incredulous. "She ran away—from *me*."

Benito jumped from the carriage, picked up the note, and smoothed it out against his thigh. He read it to himself.

Don Carlos, Sir: I regret I cannot honor my commitment to marry you. As soon as I am able, I will try to pay back what you consider your investment. I fear that a marriage between us would only lead to heartache. I do not love you, sir, and I do not wish to bind myself forever in a loveless marriage. I wish you God's speed back to your ranch. Reyna Maria Alvaron.

"Tsk. Tsk." Governor Claiborne patted Don Carlos's back in a chummy show of sympathy. "We'll send out a search party immediately. There aren't too many places a girl can hide in New Orleans, and I doubt she's had time to make contact with Lafitte's scoundrels."

Sister crossed herself and squeezed her eyes shut. "This is all my fault," she said. "If she gets hurt . . ."

Mrs. Claiborne appeared at the nun's side, and led her to a corner in the sunroom, away from the men.

"Hush now, we'll have coffee and get dressed. Reyna will be fine."

"Come inside," urged the governor once again, but the Spaniard hesitated.

Benito marveled that Don Carlos was holding his temper as well as he was. He knew his friend well. *El Capitan* would never fully recover from this new humiliation.

Yet joy surged through Benito, too, for he was well aware Don Carlos would not want the girl now. He would save face by discarding her as if she were a loose thread on his best jacket.

Don Carlos shook the governor's hand. "I will not wait a second more or spend a penny more in trying to wed that ungrateful little wench. I am most grateful for your hospitality. Good luck against the British. Benito, let's go."

Benito stepped forward, a worried frown disguising his usual optimistic good looks. "I don't think we should leave her like this, *El Capitan*. Let me stay. I want to search for her."

The older man glared at him. "Ah yes, I thought I saw sparks flying between the two of you. My old friend! *Compadre!* Trying to steal my bride-to-be! Rewarding my years of generosity with disloyalty and betrayal!"

Don Carlos's angry eyes and hurtful words cut a deep swath through Benito's soul. The young man worshiped *El Capitan,* and now he had become his enemy—all because of a girl!

"I am attracted to Reyna," Benito admitted. "But I would never have said anything, you know that— had the engagement gone as you anticipated. Now, I would like to have the freedom, and your permission, to seek her for myself."

Don Carlos stared at the ground silently for a moment. "You have turned against me, thus proving you will never rise above your barnyard beginnings. This girl, she has no class at all, an orphan brat who spits in the face of one who would care for her and protect her. You deserve each other!"

Benito was stunned by the force of his friend's anger. Did he mean these words or was this a means of preserving his dignity?

Don Carlos climbed into the driver's seat and coaxed the horses to turn. Benito grabbed at the reins as if to stop him. The older man kicked at him, aiming for his shoulder, shoving Benito backward so that he landed, sprawling, in the mud.

Benito braced himself on his elbows but did not rise. Don Carlos looked down upon the boy who had once saved his life.

"You disgust me, Benito. I had such plans for us. The north five-hundred acres. We walked the line and placed the markers together—the land for *your* ranch, for *your* herds. Gone now. And for what? A spoiled minx who thinks she is too good for me. For *me*!"

Benito stood and brushed at the mud on his soiled trousers.

"You know, boy, I'm not the kind of man who goes back on my word. The land is still yours—with or without Senorita Alvaron. But I pray you return to the Anchorage without her. As lovely as she is, she turns my stomach! I shall find a woman, not a child, to wed, and I'll be thankful every day that Reyna is not mine to control. *Hasta luego, amigo.*"

"*Vaya con Dios,*" Benito answered.

Don Carlos popped a whip over the horses' heads

and the carriage rolled out of the courtyard at a brisk pace.

Benito, his hat held in front of him, followed the governor indoors. *I will find Reyna by nightfall,* he assured himself, *and I will declare my love.*

Chapter 36

"**M**adame Poreau?" Reyna greeted the short, plump matron who bustled into the drawing room. She had been preceded only moments before by the maid, Florence, who admonished the girl: "Mind your manners! The missus is comin'."

The woman who came in wore her graying blond hair pulled tightly into a tidy bun on the crown of her head. Clear-blue eyes flashed with intelligence and wit. She grabbed Reyna's shoulders and turned her toward the light that streamed in from the street-side windows.

"You've caught a cold, haven't you? I'm not surprised—out on the levee at midnight in a pouring-down rain. Hush now, here's a hanky. Don't tell me who you are. Let me guess."

"I am . . ." Reyna rubbed a hand across gritty red-rimmed eyes.

"No, shhh! Let me show off. You are the lovely young woman from Spain who has been staying with the Claibornes this past month. Kidnapped by pirates, held against your will, escaped to New Orleans, and taken in by the governor. Then that boor of a rancher from Tejas arrived and you ran away. Foolish girl!''

''I ... yes, ma'am. You're close to having the facts right. I didn't escape from Grand Terre, though. I was sent to New Orleans to warn the governor about British ships in the Gulf of Mexico. But he sent for Don Carlos to come get me and ...''

''Wait, child. I want to hear it all, I promise you that. I'm the queen of gossip in the Crescent City, but first things first. Here, sit by me.''

''But how did you know that I'd run away from Don Carlos?'' Reyna asked her.

''Oh, I'm a sly one. Early this morning, the governor sent guards house-to-house searching for you. I discreetly asked what you looked like—and, of course the description fit exactly that of the drowned mouse who showed up on my doorstep during the night. I couldn't be *absolutely* sure, you understand, so I didn't bother to mention you.''

''It was good of you to take me in, madame.''

''My maid, Florence, is the niece of old Micah. He lives here when he's not down to the cafe. His boy, Samson, is a good man. Joincd right up in a Men of Color army unit soon as the governor asked for volunteers. Micah knew you'd be safe with me.''

Florence reentered, carrying a tray laden with coffee and cups, sugar and cream, small squares of cake, eating utensils, and linen napkins.

Madame Poreau served Reyna and engaged her in light social chitchat until she had consumed two shortbreads and a refill of coffee. The woman placed her empty cup on the cherrywood table next to the sofa, smoothed her starched skirts, then leaned back as if to say, now I'm ready. ''Tell me why you re-

136

fused to marry the wealthy Spaniard? Had he not sent for you, all the way from Spain?''

"Madame, he was insufferable! So proud and arrogant and . . .'' Reyna sputtered.

"Yes, I see. He left the city this morning, you know.''

"He left?''

"Yes, drove out of here in a very big hurry to get back home.''

Had Benito gone with him? Reyna could not ask.

Madame reached over and patted the girl's knee. "Mrs. Claiborne and Sister Augustine must be very anxious about your safety. Don't you think I should send someone over to tell them you are all right?''

"Yes, I suppose so. I don't want them to worry needlessly, but Madame, what am I to do? I don't want to go back there to live. Can you get me in touch with Lafitte? I'd rather be with Jean and Catherine than anyone else.''

"Child! You will stay here as my guest until we get this all ironed out. It would be terribly inappropriate for me to send you back to those vile scoundrels. They're in hiding, you know, skipping around the swamps one step ahead of the law.''

"Catherine is probably with her mother, and I know they live somewhere near the city. Perhaps I could stay with her?''

Madame Poreau rose and placed her hands on ample hips. "That is definitely not possible! She is a quadroon, a woman of color, and she is a concubine! And so is her sister. The mother and both daughters are thick as thieves with the Lafittes. No, that won't do at all! You will remain here with me. Now, honey, it's settled. No more discussion. Florence, send a girl over to the Claibornes' to let them know Reyna is safe. She will be staying here with us."

When Reyna went downstairs after her siesta, Florence greeted her with a bundle of dresses. "The governor's lady sent these over. Best get gussied up. They's coming a-calling at five today."

Reyna assumed the maid meant Mrs. Claiborne and Sister Augustine, so she again dressed and primped in hopes of convincing them of her complete well-being. She prayed they wouldn't be too angry because she had spurned Don Carlos.

On the dot of five o'clock, Florence admitted Reyna's guests. The nun swung Reyna around in such a fierce embrace that the girl failed to recognize the person standing a few steps behind Sister.

"I am so glad you are unharmed, dear Reyna. It's all my fault. You thought I had abandoned you, but I wouldn't do that. I never considered you might balk at marrying the Don. I failed you, child. I am so sorry!"

"It's not your fault," Reyna began. "It was that man, Don Carlos. I could not see myself wed to him and listening to his elaborate boasts for the rest of my life."

"Don Carlos has earned the right to boast," said Benito, startling Reyna who, until then, had been unaware of his presence.

"You? I won't go with you," she said fiercely. "If you remained in New Orleans so you could take me back to him, you shouldn't have. I won't go! I won't!" Reyna stomped her foot to emphasize her determination.

"Whoa!" said Benito. "You don't understand."

Sister Augustine grabbed Reyna's hand. "But I understand," she said. "Take me to your room so we can talk privately. I have much to tell you."

Chapter 37

A bewildered but beautiful Reyna sat at the grand banquet table at dinner that evening. She had packed off one suitor, and another had magically appeared.

It was a strange group, with Madame Poreau keeping up a steady patter of New Orleans society gossip as Sister Augustine smiled benevolently.

Reyna was careful that her eyes never strayed toward Benito, and, likewise, she sensed that his eyes were averted from her. Shy, their heads bowed over their plates, it seemed each one tried hard to not show any interest in the other.

After a dessert of banana flambé, Madame Poreau suggested the two young people take an evening stroll along the levee. Sister stepped forward to chaperon, but Madame detained her. "Give these young people a chance to talk," Madame said. "They won't go far and I'll have Samson trail along behind. Reyna is safe with that young man. He adores her. I can tell!"

Reyna frowned. Madame caught the look. "Now go on," she said, and shooed them out the door.

Benito, at age twenty-two, cut a fine leg, as Florence put it to Madame in a not-so-discreet aside. He was dressed in white wool pants and a navy-blue double-breasted jacket, but he looked uncomfortable in the formal attire.

Reyna, wrapped in the torn emerald cloak, walked apart from him, but was always aware of him. She cut her eyes at Benito whenever she thought he might be looking elsewhere. He walked with his hands clutched behind his back. She held hers in front of her and fiddled with a lace-trimmed handkerchief.

The night air was cool and crisp. The bad weather of the night before had moved on—swept away, Madame Poreau said, by the winds of war.

"I don't quite know how to go about this, senorita," he began. "Never before have I approached a lady such as yourself. I am not wealthy, nor do I come from the class of landowners. I own nothing but my good name and the promise of what is to come. All that I know I learned at the feet of Don Carlos. He is . . . was my best friend." He paused.

Reyna lifted her gaze to study his face, for his voice trembled with emotion. When she didn't speak, he reached out and cupped her hands gently in his own as if he were holding a small but precious treasure.

"I do not wish to rush you into any decision, for I have no idea what is going through your mind at this moment. I expect you need time to think."

The girl nodded, still silent.

Benito hurried on to finish his speech as if he had it memorized.

"Reyna Maria, I was attracted to you from the first moment we met. I became an observer, for that was my role while Don Carlos pursued you. Often I could not sleep for thinking about how you would live in the hacienda and I in the vaqueros' barracks, how you would be so near to me yet married to my best friend. I toyed with the idea of leaving the ranch, going west or back to the sea. But now . . .

"*El Capitan* has given up all title to you. I have his permission to seek your favors. He has promised me land and a herd so I am not completely without property and a means to support you, if . . . well, if you agree to marry me and we return to Tejas."

When she started to say something, he rushed on. "Wait. I am not finished, and if I don't say it now, I might not ever. I am mestizo, raised in poverty, earning my manhood by besting others in fights and trades. And you . . . you are . . . like a jewel, rare and beautiful. But it is not simply your beauty that enthralls me, senorita—it is your spirit. How do I say this? I do not wish to own you but rather to share my life with you. I will honor you, Reyna, always. I will care for you and treasure you. I would give my life for you."

Benito lifted Reyna's hand and brushed his lips across it, then he released her and resumed walking slowly, a step or two in front of her. He seemed embarrassed.

Touched by his words, Reyna considered herself to be standing poised on a precipice. *How can I accept him or reject him? I have so much unfinished business,* she thought. *What about Lafitte? And Jules? Did they really abandon me? Or are they in trouble and cannot reach me? What of the British who lurk so close by? Do I not owe allegiance to this new land? How can I run away when war threatens my new friends?*

The darkness soaked up Benito's nervousness like

a sponge. She knew he was waiting for her to speak, to indicate if there was any chance she might allow him to woo her.

This Benito is attractive and he is sincere and I find myself drawn to him like a moth to a flame. But this is happening too quickly. I do not know my own mind. What shall I say?

"Benito?" Her voice floated on the air like an angel's whisper.

Ten steps away, he turned. His look embraced her in the moonlight.

"Benito, I am not of the aristocracy. I bring you no dowry. I am an orphan."

"It does not matter, my love."

"I do not wish to be courted in the old-fashioned way—treated like an object rather than a person."

"I will do your bidding, whatever it be."

"I will not be set upon a pedestal and treated like a statue of clay, with no wit or will of my own."

"I will worship you for who you are."

Reyna paused, shocked by the currents of joy that suddenly vibrated through her. *Maybe he is the right man for me. Maybe God sent him! But this is the wrong time. I have obligations.* "Benito," she said, "I am willing to see where this might lead, but I have commitments—Sister Augustine, Jean Lafitte, this brave new land of America."

"*Si*, I understand, but war is coming," he said. "It is a risk to remain in New Orleans much longer."

"But I *must* stay! I doubt you will understand my reasoning. I'm not sure I understand it myself."

The girl wrung her hands as she carefully chose her words. "I have always been under the authority of someone else. The nuns and priests at the convent,

Sister Augustine, the master of the Spanish ship, the pirates, the governor, Don Carlos.

"All of my life, someone else has been telling me what to do, and how to think."

She licked dry lips as she searched for the right words. "When I ran away from Don Carlos, I probably made a terrible mistake."

Benito's face drained of color and expression.

"No, no, that's not what I mean. I'm trying to say that I should have stood up to him, stood up to everyone. I knew the first day he came that I would not be happy as his wife. I knew then, too . . . that I felt a stirring inside me, a pull . . . toward you."

She lowered her eyes. Benito leaned closer. Samson's clothing rustled as he stepped from foot to foot, far enough away not to overhear, but close enough should the girl need him.

Reyna rubbed her forehead as if she could coax the words from her brain, express ideas she had never spoken aloud before. "I must stay here. I must not run away again. I want to be my own person before I pledge myself to another in marriage."

Her eyes pleaded with him, but her voice held steady. "Benito, if you want to remain here, if you will agree to give me time—I will be very pleased. But if you leave, I will understand. If you leave, you leave without me."

Chapter 38

November 1814

Reyna continued to reside with Madame Poreau and quickly was caught up in the preparations for war. She helped collect medical supplies, bandages, food, and jugs of water to quench thirst.

Her days were long and hard as she slaved alongside the other New Orleans women, including the governor's wife, who had refused to retreat to northern Louisiana. Reyna's knuckles bled from scrubbing petticoats to bind the wounds of American warriors. Her eyes were frequently teary—not from emotion—but from peeling onions.

Often she reflected on the mood of the city as it girded itself for war. Rowdy New Orleans had taken on a somber personality. The men who trudged through the muddy streets were often tired and worn from walking miles to join the American forces. Some were battle-weary from the recent Indian wars; others were fresh-faced mountain boys from Kentucky and Tennessee, hungering for their first taste of blood.

Reyna thought Benito wore his new uniform proudly. He had not wasted a day before signing up for the volunteer militia. He had taken her mission as his own. She liked to watch him march through the city's bogs during daily drills that were supposed to ready untried troops for battle with seasoned British veterans.

Trumpets blared orders to charge and to retreat and, when she heard them, she shivered with a premonition of disaster. She and Benito were fast becoming friends, for Reyna wanted desperately to know him as a friend before she considered him as a suitor. Some days they only caught glimpses of each other. Still they managed to find moments to share.

It was always in the midnight hours that a persistent thought awakened her. *Am I sending Benito into a slaughter?* Never had she insisted that he join up with the American forces. But by refusing to leave with him, she might have unwittingly manipulated him into a position where he had to stay and fight.

One evening, Madame Poreau and Reyna joined Benito at the army camp near the levee, and blended their soprano voices with his tenor in the rollicking songs of war. That was the night she first heard a haunting new war song, written only last September—at the Battle of Ft. McHenry in Baltimore.

The young sailor, who had only recently reached New Orleans, preceded his singing with an explanation of how the song had come to be. Several months ago, a Maryland lawyer, Francis Scott Key, was detained aboard a ship in Baltimore harbor the night the British attacked. The bombardment, loud and heavy, lasted all night long.

At dawn, when Key saw that the United States

flag still flew over the fort, he was inspired to pen the lines of a song, which immediately was set to the music of an old English anthem, "Anacreon in Heaven."

The sailor told the people sitting around the campfire that the song had become popular overnight. Softly, with only an artificial drumroll provided by a spoon on the bottom of a tin pan, the boy accompanied himself as he sang slowly and plaintively:

> *Oh, say can you see,*
> *By the dawn's early light,*
> *What so proudly we hailed*
> *At the twilight's last gleaming?*
>
> *Whose broad stripes and bright stars,*
> *Through the perilous fight,*
> *O'er the ramparts we watched,*
> *Were so gallantly streaming!*
>
> *And the rockets' red glare,*
> *The bombs bursting in air,*
> *Gave proof through the night*
> *That our flag was still there.*

The young man stood abruptly, removed his sailor's cap and placed it over his heart. His eyes stared into the starry distance as if privileged to see some private awe-inspiring sight. His voice took on a timbre of devotion and grew in volume and strength.

> *O' say, does that Star-Spangled*
> *Banner yet wave*
> *O'er the land of the free*
> *And the home of the brave?*

Joined by others who knew the tune, but did not know the words, he led the group in the second verse. They all joined in on the chorus.

> *'Tis the Star-Spangled Banner*
> *Oh, long may it wave.*
> *O'er the land of the free*
> *And the home of the brave.*

Reyna felt a chill—fear or pride? Perhaps neither, maybe both. *I belong here,* she thought.

She glanced at Benito, his brown Mexican skin glowing golden in the firelight. The expression on his face, one of fierce determination and pride, was repeated on face after face around the camp circle.

Chapter 39

December 2, 1814

When Reyna first saw Andrew Jackson, she thought he would fall out of his saddle before he reached St. Louis Square.

Reyna was concerned. General Jackson, their savior, seemed barely able to walk without support. He was bony and thin, his skin yellowed, his sallow hawk-like face a mask of the man she expected to see.

Jackson suffered from malaria, contracted in the Alabama swamps while fighting Indian uprisings. He obviously was tired from the weeks of battling with savages. Now he faced another difficult campaign, one that many said was doomed to disaster.

The governor hastily arranged for army headquarters to be set up on Royal Street, then invited the general to rest at his house. A dinner and meeting would be held that night, attended by the mayor, Commodore Patterson, and several other local patriots. Reyna was visiting Mrs. Claiborne when the general arrived at the mansion. She stood at the door as he entered, curtsied after a brief introduction, and relieved him of his threadbare blue Spanish cloak. She couldn't help but notice the mud spatters on the coat and his high dragoon boots.

He wore a tired, sad expression as he followed Mrs. Claiborne to the upstairs front bedroom that Reyna had once occupied.

But when General Jackson descended the staircase for dinner, he wore a new, clean and well-fitted uniform. His face, no longer haggard. His eyes, bright and alert. His manners, impeccable. Reyna was amazed at the transformation.

She eavesdropped while she helped serve the five-course meal. It didn't take long for General Jackson to find out about the pitifully small navy, and the weak Fort St. Phillip, seventy-five miles below New Orleans on the Mississippi. As yet, Fort Petites Coquilles on the Bayou Rigolets was unfinished.

He would command an army of seven-hundred regulars, and a large untrained but dedicated group of volunteers. The governor complained about inadequate arms, a skimpy supply of ammunition, and a severe shortage of flints, which rendered useless the few weapons the Americans did have.

Twelve thousand hand-picked, seasoned soldiers of the British Army were on their way to take possession of New Orleans. Was his a hopeless task? Could General Jackson work a miracle?

During the meal, Reyna noticed how courteous and gentlemanly he treated the ladies, how cordial and clever he was with the men. And when the politicoes retired from the dinner table to go to the drawing room for drinks and talk of war, Jackson bridled with feverish energy.

The man must be under a great deal of pressure,

Reyna knew. *British troops could be on American soil before he even has time to organize his paltry forces.*

By listening to Governor Claiborne and the "Queen of Gossip," Madame Poreau, Reyna learned that during the course of the following day General Andrew Jackson inspected and ordered improvements at Ft. St. Phillip, established fortifications at other possible points of invasion, and ordered that all canals and bayous giving access to New Orleans be permanently blocked.

On the evening of the general's second day in the Crescent City, Mrs. Claiborne asked Reyna to carry a dinner tray to him at army headquarters, where his office had become his living quarters as well.

Reyna tapped on the outer door, but no one answered. She pulled it open, balancing the dinner tray on one knee. The main hall was deserted. The general was stretched out on a sofa in a small room adjoining the headquarters' office. His eyes were half-closed, and he shivered with chills. Reyna could see that his body was wracked by pain.

Lightly she tapped on the door jamb, not wanting to disturb him, but certain he needed the food she brought if he was to remain alive.

General Jackson cracked open one eye and looked at her. With an effort, he rose from the sofa and took the tray. "Thank you, Miss Reyna."

General Jackson remembered my name!

"Won't you sit with me a spell?" he asked. "I tire of looking at my battle-weary companions."

She poured him a cup of hot tea, then sat in a straight-backed chair next to the large table that served as his desk.

He ate with fervor and bragged of the food's tastiness. "I expect I can go on now. Thank you for the sustenance and the pleasure of your company."

Reyna assumed she had been dismissed so she stood and prepared to take his tray. She hesitated when he sighed and sank into his chair, his head bent back, his knotty throat exposed. Then his head fell forward and he sighed again.

"I am weary, oh so weary," he said. "Our task is almost insurmountable. Seven-hundred regulars against as many as fifteen-thousand men. I'm told they left Ireland early in September bound for the Louisiana coast. I am being indiscreet, I know, but I tell you this, young lady, I will burn this city before I allow it to fall into the hands of the enemy."

"We are not defeated yet." Reyna spoke with the vigor of youth.

General Jackson seemed to drop his defenses as he rested his head in his hands. There was complete silence for several minutes, and she wondered if he had forgotten she was there.

Seeing New Orleans's savior appear so defeated, Reyna felt a rod of resolve stiffen her backbone. She decided to speak now and worry later if she had offended the war hero.

"General, sir," she began, "I'd like to make a suggestion. It is not one that will gain approval from Governor Claiborne and his cabinet, though, for it has been mentioned to them before."

"Ah." He leaned his desk chair back against the wall and stretched his long legs in front of him. "You think you have a way out of this dilemma, my child? Let me hear it. And even if it has been suggested before, it is likely it did not reach my ears." He encouraged her with a polite but vacant smile.

He is only being nice to me because I am female, and because he is bone-weary and at a dead-end.

"Well," she said, "perhaps you have heard of the privateer, Jean Lafitte, and his brother, Pierre? They are considered outlaws, and they have been treated very shabbily by the governor's administration." Reyna told him about the warships and the letters from the British and how Lafitte had sent her to warn the governor. With vehemence, she explained how the warnings had been disregarded and, instead, Governor Claiborne had sent his men to capture Lafitte and his treasures.

General Jackson allowed his chair to fall forward with a thump. "What are you getting at, miss? Would you that the American forces take in a motley crew of thieves and murderers? How do I know they can be trusted? How do I know they won't betray us to the British?"

Reyna pulled herself up to her full height and spoke with an eloquence she did not know she possessed.

"General Jackson, I know for a fact that the Lafittes own a treasure trove of guns and munitions and precious flints for which you would probably give your right arm. Yet, because these men operate a successful business outside the jurisdiction of Louisiana courts, and because they do not pay taxes to a government that refuses to acknowledge them, you will ignore their help?"

She raised praying hands to her mouth, then solemnly continued. "You will turn down their gift of flints and guns and cannon? You will disregard the service of these experienced fighters? Tell me, sir, where are *your* priorities? All these men ask is to be pardoned for past crimes. They are eager to help save this state, this nation.''

Reyna picked up the tray. Exasperated, she shook her head. ''I simply do not understand men!''

General Jackson plunged forward and barred the door with his braced arm. ''Wait,'' he said. ''Let me think this through. You are telling me there is a cache of flints hidden somewhere in the swamps and it is accessible to us immediately if I pardon the Lafittes?''

''That is it exactly, General, sir.''

He rested one of his massive hands on Reyna's shoulder and held the other one high over his head in a sign of praise. ''Thank God and Jean Lafitte! When can you arrange a meeting?''

Reyna found Benito at the farmers' market near the levee.

''Benito, I need you. I need your help desperately!''

The young man flashed a radiant white smile. *''Caramba!* at last, she really needs me!''

''Don't be silly,'' she scolded. ''I need you to find Jean Lafitte. You did it once before. You know, when you killed Tomas.''

At his pained expression, Reyna hurried to say, ''I'm sorry, that's not what I really meant. It's just that there's a chance Jean can save New Orleans with all the weapons and flints he has hoarded. General Jackson is willing to pardon him in exchange for his help against the British.''

''Dios mio!'' Benito said. ''You have been a busy young lady—changing the face of the war, when I thought you were just serving *el viejo,* the old man, his dinner.''

''Please,'' she begged. ''Please help me find them. Jean and Pierre, Picou and Jules. I need them all here

for a meeting tomorrow. It's six o'clock now. Can
we do it? I mean, can you do it?''

"I'm glad you never ask the impossible. All you
want is for me to locate a band of cutthroats who
hide in the Louisiana bayous and are determined not
to be found. And it is already dark. A small task.''
He grinned at her.

"Please, Benito, don't tease me. This is really
important.''

"I know, *mi corazon*. Let us put our heads together. I'll contact all the swamp rats I can find. I've
heard Lafitte is holed up near the city, living in luxury. He is not as isolated as you think.''

"You did not tell me this before,'' she said
accusingly.

Benito shrugged. "It's only a rumor. You visit the
coffeehouses and spread the word that General Jackson is asking after Jean Lafitte. We'll hit both ends
of New Orleans society. Surely, someone will know
how to find him.''

The next morning, Benito Sandoval rode out of
the swamps, mosquito bitten and smeared with black
gumbo mud, but he wore a satisfied smile.

He bathed and changed clothes before he knocked
at the gate of the Poreau house and inquired for
Reyna, who at once asked, "Did you find him?''

He greeted her with a discreet kiss on her hand.

"Aye,'' he said, with a mischievous glint. "The
pirate king is willing to meet the American general
at the public coffeehouse on the square at high noon.
He suggested we arrange for a private room on the
second floor.''

Reyna hugged Benito. "I am so happy. Is he well?
Jean, I mean? Did you see Picou and Catherine?

What about Jules? Are they all coming? Can I come, too?''

"Ah, *mi amor,* my love. Yes to everything except the last question. You would be out of place at such a meeting, unless . . . unless you were there to serve."

Reyna was indignant. "This was all my idea! But no matter. I'd wash their feet if it would get me into the same room with my old friends."

"Uh, Reyna?" Benito said, suddenly serious. "I don't have to worry, do I? You know, about Jules or Jean? About you?"

"You goose! This is about government and war and secret alliances. It has nothing to do with childish romance. Besides, don't you trust me?"

Benito shrugged his shoulders, but the light disappeared from his eyes, and his mouth was set in sad resolve.

Chapter 40

A well-dressed, relaxed, and handsome Jean Lafitte and his lieutenants, Jules LeFevre, Picou, and Father Francis, reined in at the coffeehouse and waited. Picou's hand rested heavily upon the musket holstered on his saddle.

Jules smiled broadly at Reyna as she hurried down the stairs to greet them. His right hand, however, never left the pistol tucked into his waistband.

Lafitte seemed less fearful of a double-cross. He sat confident and tall, and he winked at Reyna when she paused near the hitching rail.

Reyna spoke first. "It's so good to see you. How's Catherine and Cara and Gabriella? I've missed you all so much."

Father Francis dismounted and blessed Reyna, as well as the men in his party. "And what of Sister Augustine?" he asked.

"She is well, Father. Living at the governor's mansion for the time being. But all she talks about is this war being over so she can go back to work with you."

Father nodded as he tied his horse to the hitching post.

Lafitte dismounted, and bussed Reyna's cheek, his hand lifting her chin so he could look into her eyes. "I understand from your Mexican friend that this meeting is all your doing."

"You aren't angry, are you? I thought ... I thought you would want to come out of hiding and help the Americans."

"Yes, my dear, I do want to be of service. But the key here rests on whether or not your General Jackson can be trusted. You will recall that once before ..."

"Oh, Jean, that was horrible! They wouldn't listen to me!"

Benito stepped forward from the ground-floor public room and stood a few feet behind Reyna. His fingers lightly played upon the hilt of a dagger sheathed at his side. When Jean glanced at him, so did Reyna. She could sense his tension. She stepped back and linked her arm with his.

"This is Benito Sandoval, whom you have already met. We are considering marriage."

Jules leaned forward from his mount. "Does this mean that we are no longer engaged?"

"Why, Jules LeFevre, we never were!"

The pirate laughed. "Did you tell your young man about our midnight trip through the bayous?"

Reyna bristled. She would not tolerate Jules's casting any aspersions on her virtue. She glared at him, and did not hold her tongue as he expected. Reyna had become bold.

"Monsieur LeFevre, Benito is well-informed about my life with the pirates of Barataria. I have done nothing of which I am ashamed. By the way, where were you, Captain LeFevre, when I needed you? You abandoned me. Disappeared. I doubt you ever even watched to see if I removed the silk scarf. Our signal, remember?''

Jules appeared nonplussed, unable to speak. Picou slapped his thigh in mirth. Father Francis smiled broadly.

"Enough," said Lafitte. "We are here on a mission of extreme importance. I am in Reyna's debt. But we must remain ever alert. This is no time for joviality. Our best intentions were rejected once before." His steely gaze rested on the girl. "Where is your general and his aides?"

"General Jackson and the governor will be here soon. The upstairs meeting room is ready. We've prepared a morsel or two—nothing as elaborate as what we served the British at Grand Terre." Reyna's eyes twinkled in remembrance. "Come on up and get comfortable. They will be here soon."

Picou slipped down from his horse. "I'm ready to eat," he said, dusting his hands on his pants.

Jean's dark eyes tracked up and down the street. "I have placed men in a circle around this coffeehouse. It would not be wise to enter just yet and be cut off from them. Jules, keep watch," he said. "I am going into the cathedral to offer up a prayer."

Reyna gulped. *I brought Lafitte to New Orleans for this meeting. What if it is a double-cross? What if the general has been influenced by the governor and his cabinet? What if armed guards are on their way here now to arrest my friends?*

"Benito?" She sensed he could read her thoughts.

"General Jackson is a man of his word," Benito said. "I will remain outside during the meeting to keep watch over the area. I will not allow anyone to sneak up on your friends."

Reyna sighed with relief when moments later General Jackson strolled across the wide boulevard accompanying Jean Lafitte, their heads bent together in conversation. They had met in the gardens of the cathedral, and now were already deep in discussion.

"These are my lieutenants," Jean said as he introduced Jules and Picou. "And my chaplain, Father Francis."

"My men should be here shortly," General Jackson said. "I've asked Governor Claiborne not to come. I felt there might be some animosity between the two of you that could hamper the business we have to do here today."

The pirates, the priest, and the American general preceded Reyna up the outside staircase. Micah joined her and trudged up the steps alongside. He would help her serve. Benito saluted Reyna and remained behind on the street. A backward glance revealed Samson and several other men of color standng nearby. They were armed. Samson tipped his hat.

Shortly after the pirates were seated, several Americans in uniform solemnly entered and stood at attention behind General Jackson. He acknowledged them and said, "At ease." They chose chairs on the general's side of the table and sat down.

Reyna served coffee while the general paced the room. He motioned for Reyna to close the shutters. "What we say here today shall remain secret until the appropriate time. Is that acceptable to you, Lafitte?"

The pirate nodded, his arms folded against his chest as he watched the American legend organize his thoughts.

General Jackson began, "I have seven-hundred men with fighting experience, and perhaps another thousand who are strictly untried volunteers. I do not know if they can be counted upon during the thick of battle. I am short on everything—supplies, guns, ammunition, flints, cannon, and cannon balls. Within the week, British soldiers and sailors, seasoned by the recent war in Europe, will invade our shores by the tens of thousands. Our only advantages are a knowledge of the geography of this place, our cool heads, sharp eyes, and our determination to win this lopsided war.''

He stopped in front of Lafitte, at parade rest. ''Reyna tells me you have the capabilities to turn this war around. She also tells me that once before you offered your help and it was not accepted, and, in fact, led to the destruction of your ... business empire. I'm wondering, sir, why you would be willing to come forward now, with yet another price on your head.'' Jackson looked around the room. ''We are gentlemen here, sir. Let us speak only the truth.''

Lafitte, always a commanding figure, stood and walked around the table so that he and the general were standing on the same side.

''Let's cut through the diplomacy and get to the heart of the matter,'' Jean said. ''I have as many as five hundred fighting men who will follow me into battle on the American side. Some of them presently are incarcerated in New Orleans's prisons. I have pistols and ammunition, cannon and lead balls, a few ships, and the one item you require more than any other—I have probably as many as seventy-five hundred pistol flints. These are all yours at a wave of my hand.''

Lafitte looked around the room to see how the others were reacting to his words. Father Francis nodded, encouraging him to continue.

"All my brother, Pierre, and I ask of you is this: to be pardoned for what the governor calls our crimes against society, although I admit no guilt, you understand. And we wish to be accepted as fellow Americans. Heretofore we have been men without a country."

General Jackson reached his massive hand toward Lafitte, who hesitated only slightly before he gripped it. The strength that passed through that handshake sealed their bargain.

Later, when the two leaders parted after a hastily eaten repast, Reyna was privy to hear General Jackson thank Lafitte for his help.

"I wish to fight alongside you, sir," said Lafitte.

"I'd be proud to have you," the general replied, "but your knowledge of the bayous may be more valuable than your shooting arm in the days to come. Today I place New Orleans under martial law. My door is always open to you, Lafitte. I welcome your cooperation."

All proceedings against the Lafitte brothers were suspended that very day. Jails were opened and Lafitte's banditti were turned loose. Smugglers were called in from bayou hideaways. Boats and wagons began to funnel much needed war supplies to American camps throughout the area.

Chapter 41

December 1814

On December 9, fifty British ships arrived on the Louisiana coast. By December 22, the British army had advanced to within nine miles of New Orleans. General Jackson learned of the British landing on the afternoon of December 23. He ordered an immediate reconnaissance and chose Pierre Lafitte to lead a brigade of Tennessee mounted riflemen to the Villere plantation and await further orders.

"We must be bold!" Jackson told his officers, striking his desk with his fist. For hours, he had poured over the maps spread across the long table that served as his desk. He had worked so tirelessly planning his campaign against the British that most of his officers were exhausted. They could not keep up with his fits of feverish energy.

Just that morning, Reyna commented to Madame Poreau that she was worried sick General Jackson might die. How could New Orleans survive without him?

The general had aged considerably in the two

weeks he'd been in the city. Sometimes she thought he had the personalities of two men. When he was with the governor or any of the New Orleans well-to-do, he was gracious and affable. He stood tall and carried himself with authority. He inspired confidence.

When he was with his men, he often looked spent. His words were harsh. He cursed in a colorful manner that brought a blush to Reyna's cheeks. General Jackson showed a low level of tolerance toward any man foolish enough to cross him.

When Reyna saw him that morning, his eyes were half-shut, his face flushed, his breathing rattled. By midafternoon, General Andrew Jackson was a battering ram of energy. He relied on his reserve strength to come up with a plan that would destroy the enemy and throw its camp into confusion.

The general ordered the Navy schooner *Carolina* to move quietly up the river so her men could bombard the British camp after dark. His plan was to catch the British off guard, to make them think they were being attacked by a formidable force. Guns aboard the *Carolina* commenced firing at about the same time the sharpshooters, under Pierre Lafitte, began to aim their long rifles and pick off Redcoats one by one.

The fight went well for the Americans, until after dark. On orders, they had moved into the British camp and engaged the British in hand-to-hand combat, but in the darkness they soon found themselves fighting each other. Reinforcements came to help the Redcoats, so the American commanding officer called for a withdrawal.

Jackson ordered his men to fall back to the Rodriguez Canal, a ditch fifteen feet wide that separated the Chalmette and Macarty plantations.

Meanwhile, he ordered his men to build a mile-long shoulder-high rampart, using mud, rails, fence posts, wooden kegs, anything they could get their hands on. The rampart was placed in a fortunate position between the Mississippi River and an impassable cypress swamp. The men called it "Line Jackson."

The American forces, which included men of every color and from many nations, worked in unison building the rampart, moving in cannon, and recovering horses, blankets, and clothing abandoned during the unsuccessful action the night before. Several miles away, in New Orleans, the womenfolk were hard at work, too, preparing medical stations, and gallons and gallons of food to be transported to the front lines. A feverish pitch of activity filled every waking hour.

Reyna and Sister Augustine visited the Ursuline Convent where schoolrooms had been turned into infirmaries for the wounded soldiers expected to soon flood their way. On the way back to St. Louis Square, Reyna walked over to a tree and plucked down a poster to read. The paper had not been there when they walked by earlier.

"What is this?" she cried, showing it to Sister Augustine. The message, written first in French, and then in Spanish, invited the people of French and Spanish descent to remain quietly in their homes, apart from the war. The poster assured them the British were only at war with the upshot Americans.

Posters were everywhere, hanging from tree trunks and fence posts and wind-scattered upon the lawns and muddy streets.

Solemnly Reyna looked at Sister. "There are traitors and spies among us," she said. "They are trying to turn our own people against us. God, how I hate them!"

"My dear," came the calming voice of Sister Augustine. "The British are human, too. They want to return a portion of the American continent to the British throne. They believe their cause is just, and they will do anything in their power to bring about victory—just as surely as we will ourselves. We must pray—pray for men on both sides—pray for their souls."

Reyna tossed her dark hair, and placed her hands on her hips. "Benito is out there, and Jean and Jules and Picou and General Jackson. I say, pray for victory!"

Chapter 42

New Orleans

The morning of January 8, 1815, was a day of fear for the women of New Orleans. They somberly arose at dawn, speaking quietly among themselves, preparing for a day that could deprive many of them of their dearest loved ones.

The British commander had been shocked when, on New Year's Day, the Americans silenced all the British guns by noon. Except for occasional sniper fire, the guns on both sides had stayed silent the next week while British and Americans prepared for the final battle.

Reyna and Sister Augustine helped Florence and Madame Poreau keep order in the big house on Royal Street. The mansion overflowed with women and young children, many of whom had arrived the night before.

Windows were barred, shutters closed. Candles burned everywhere—for light and for their men. Women in prayer knelt throughout the house, in groups and privately.

Before dawn, Reyna wakened to a new sound—an unusual sound, yet one that reminded her of her youth. In the dark it seemed unidentifiable, until she accidentally stumbled over a young girl in prayer. Then she recognized the sound—the click of rosary beads moving through dozens of hands throughout both floors of the Poreau mansion. It was the sound that had accompanied her growing-up years at the convent.

At dawn, the noise of cannonade rumbled across the city—as loud and out-of-place as thunder on a clear winter's day.

If I didn't know better, Reyna thought, *I'd say the world was coming to an end. If Benito dies, it will have come to an end for me.*

She tried frantically to calm the women around her. She helped Florence in the kitchen until midday, when she slipped out of the house and hurried to the Ursuline Convent to see how Sister Augustine was bearing up.

The noise of battle was much louder outside. She could see smoke in the far-off distance. So many of the trees in the square had lost their leaves to winter. Their naked branches seemed to reach up in supplication to their creator.

At the convent, she found the sisters had moved a statue in front of their door, to bar the enemy. Sister Augustine was around back, listlessly peering into an iron pot of boiling water. Sister wiped her face and turned with Reyna to face the Chalmette plains.

"If he dies, I am dead," Reyna said.

"If the British win, we all are dead," came Sister's sharp-tongued reply.

Reyna's face blanched. "General Jackson will raze the city before he allows the British to come here."

Sister made the sign of the cross. "General Jackson is not God," she said. "He may not be able to save us."

Reyna hugged the nun, and they kissed as would a mother and daughter in farewell. "I must go back," Reyna said, "I am needed at Madame's."

"Go with God," Sister said quietly. "*Vaya con Dios.*"

Reyna heard the shrieks and wails before she reached the house. Every building in the French Quarter seemed to vibrate with the sounds of women weeping.

When she entered Madame Poreau's she found the household out of control. The women were hysterical, crying, fainting, being stepped on and over by others who had gone mad with fear.

Where is Madame? I must do something about this.

"Come, come." Reyna shouted to get their attention. "We cannot fall apart while our men are on the battlefield defending our homeland. We must get organized. There is much to be done. Where is Madame Poreau?"

Florence bustled forward. "Thank God, you're here. I didn't know what to do."

"What happened?"

"The governor's wife sent for Madame—to sit with her over to the mansion. Without her, everybody's done gone crazy!"

"Now. Now. It's going to be all right," Reyna said. "First, how many of you know how to use weapons? How many would be willing to fire on the enemy?"

At a small show of hands, Reyna selected a rawboned Cajun woman to be in charge of defenses. "Do whatever you deem necessary to protect this house and its occupants," she told her.

"Now who among you will take care of our children, so that other mothers will be free?"

Several young women stepped forward and led the children, ages seven and under, to a bright light-filled bedroom at the back of the house on the second story. They placed mattresses over the windows to further protect the room and its occupants.

"Florence, you and Micah are in charge of the kitchen. We will need food for our guests, and we should be making plans for our returning victors." A few smiles appeared around the room.

"The rest of us have no specific duties. We will do whatever must be done. If it is to bind the wounds of a young soldier who has lost his eyes or his legs, we will do it. If it is to wrap the dead bodies of those we love, we will do it. If it is to set fire to our homes and destroy our supplies, we will do it to prevent the British from taking anything that is ours.

"In the meantime, we will pray, we will work, and we will gird ourselves with the same strength and determination that our men wear on yon fields of blood."

Later, when the women were calmer and going about their assigned tasks, Reyna slipped upstairs and removed from a dainty enameled box on her dresser the emerald Jules had given her. She pinned it inside her camisole. The emerald could buy food. It could buy passage to Tejas or further west. It could be payment for a herd of cattle—or it could be a bribe to save Benito's life.

* * *

By late afternoon, the sudden quiet, replacing the incessant sounds of battle, frightened the people inside the Poreau mansion.

"It is over," Reyna said simply, "but we still must wait to hear the outcome."

"What if . . . ?" began one woman, her voice building toward hysteria.

Reyna hushed her. "General Jackson will not leave us waiting for long. He will send news."

Within an hour, Madame Poreau beat upon the front door of her own home and shouted, "Someone's coming!"

The women opened the shutters, and rushed out into the street and onto the balcony.

Reyna watched the lone horseman gallop down the deserted street toward them. The young man drew rein on his foam-flecked horse. The stallion reared, and the boy waved his hat at the women.

"Victory! Victory!" he shouted.

That was all they needed to know.

It was later when Reyna's doubts set in.

Carriages loaded with medical supplies, food, and anxious women ran helter-skelter down the dirt ruts toward Chalmette. Micah hitched up Madame's brass-trimmed buggy. Florence boarded, then Micah suggested Reyna join them on the trip to the battlefield. Madame Poreau had already left with Mrs. Claiborne and the governor.

"No," Reyna said. "You go on. I'll wait here. There's still much to do."

"Ain't you being a martyr, Miss Reyna?" asked Florence. "Ain't you just dying to find that Mex'can man and throw your arms around him?"

"If I ever see him again, I will do just that," she

170

said, "and I will never let him go. But I'm not as brave as some," Reyna added. "I can't face *not* finding him. Look for Benito, please. Tell him I'm waiting. Send him home to me."

Chapter 43

It was almost dark when the first wagons of wounded appeared on the streets of New Orleans. The Poreau house was agleam with lights, and Reyna watched, with wide eyes, from the front stoop. One by one, the wagons, carrying both British and American wounded, churned down the lanes toward the convent's hastily set-up infirmary. Men and boys, mud splattered and weary, some bearing bloody injuries, walked alongside the wagons, while others hung out of the windows of the returning carriages.

Reyna was beside herself with worry. Where was Benito? Where were Micah and Florence? What about her pirate friends? And what of General Jackson himself? Shouldn't he be returning to the city amid shouts and glory? She was sorry she hadn't gone to the battlefield.

Knowing has to be better than not knowing, she thought. *I've come so far, dear God. I've come so far. And for what?*

Reyna lifted her face to the heavens and wailed as if her heart were broken. "Why did You bring me here, if You were going to take away the only thing that matters to me?''

''And what is that?'' The voice came out of the darkness—and for a moment, Reyna wondered if God had spoken aloud to her.

She hid her eyes, and whispered, ''Is it you, Benito?''

''*Si, mi alma,* it is I.''

''Thank God, you survived. Thank God, we defeated them.'' But Reyna could not make herself look at the man to whom she had given her heart. Quietly, her eyes still averted, she asked, ''Benito, are you hurt?''

''Would it matter to you if I am not whole?''

Reyna threw herself into Benito's arms, running her hands over his face, across his chest, from shoulders to hands. He surrounded her with love, his strength flowed into her. Silently she thanked God again for keeping her young warrior safe.

Reyna was no longer a child, no longer a victim of circumstance. And she no longer would live a life determined by the whims of others.

Assured Benito had escaped injury, she pulled away slightly, and undid the emerald brooch inside the bodice of her gown.

''Our future,'' she said as she pressed it into his hand and wrapped his fist around it.

''Our future?'' he said. ''What will it be? New Orleans, Tejas, the great American west?''

''Shhhh! At this moment, the only thing that matters . . .'' She interrupted him with a kiss.

Benito scooped her into his arms. Her head rested upon his shoulder as she plucked a piece of cane straw from his dark hair.

"As I was saying, the only thing that matters now is that you are here with me," she said.

"And we will wed and live together, my darling, *siempre eternidad*," he whispered. "In the land of the free and the home of the brave."

If you enjoyed *Reyna's Reward*,

sample the following brief selection from

Sofia's Heart,

the next historical adventure in

American Dreams,

coming in November 1996 from Avon Flare

When Sofia and her father arrived at the Custom House, they were greeted by noise and activity. Since the thick-walled building was the first processing point in Alta, California, all ships that were trading with the northern inhabitants of Alta had to stop and declare their goods here. The waters around the small dock were shallow, so the cargo had to be brought in by small boats. The goods were either deposited here or checked and returned to each ship to be carried on to San Francisco. The process took a long time.

Sofia liked the activity at the Custom House. Not only were the boxes and trunks full of orders for merchants and the military, but many traders brought in their goods to be sold directly to the local residents and those from the nearby ranchos. The area was brimming with Spanish men with their dark, broad-brimmed hats, short jackets, and black breeches trimmed with glittering braids and buttons. The Spanish women, on the other hand, demanded vivid color in their clothing. And although they admired European styles, they generally did without corsets and bloused their dresses and left their arms bare. In spite of Sofia's preference for a more conservative style of dress, she loved the Spanish mix of color and texture. She especially loved the fancy high combs the women wore in their dark hair from which draped delicate lace shawls or mantillas.

Señor DuFay went to work, sorting through the piles of cargo, and talking to the crew and traders about his orders. He and Sofia opened each box carefully and went through the contents to see that everything listed and requested was in good order before he paid the bill. Sofia never failed to marvel at the brisk businesslike manner of her gentle father when he was at the Custom House. Nothing escaped his discerning eye. Some of the hearty crew members loaded Señor DuFay's goods onto his wagon while he counted out the payment for each order. Sofia, acting as his assistant, carefully wrote down each transaction in a large ledger. The DuFays were just finishing up when Sofia felt a tap on her shoulder. She turned around to find Estrella smiling at her.

"Isn't it wonderful, Sofia . . . all this commotion?" Estrella's dark eyes flashed with excitement.

"I thought you liked peace and quiet," Sofia said with a laugh.

"Oh, this is different from my house," Estrella protested. "Have you ever seen such handsome young men?"

She turned and made a sweeping gesture toward the swarm of sailors in their berets, striped shirts, and tight pants, their muscled backs tossing the cargo from one person to the next.

Sofia smiled at her friend and gazed around the busy harbor. Then, suddenly, her eyes rested on a young man standing next to Isabela Palafox. He was taller than Señor DuFay, with a straight back and broad shoulders. He was dressed in a dark, unadorned suit with a short jacket. The white shirt beneath was open at the neck. He was hatless and a lock of thick, dark hair fell across his brow. Even from the distance, Sofia could see that his dark eyes were full of laughter.

"Oh, you've noticed Antonio," Estrella said, following Sofia's gaze. "Isn't he handsome? And he is just as nice as he always was." She dropped her voice. "He is so different from Isabela."

Sofia did not respond to Estrella's comments. Her eyes were still fixed on the young Palafox heir. She had felt a sudden lurch in her chest when she looked at him, something she had never before experienced.

"Come, Sofia, I want you to meet him." Estrella grabbed Sofia by the arm before she could protest and pulled her through the crowd to where Isabella and her brother were standing.

"Antonio," Estrella said cheerfully, "I want you to meet my friend, Sofia DuFay." She glanced at Isabela and shrugged slightly. "She's Isabela's friend, too, of course."

Sofia was never so grateful for her dark skin. At least it did not betray the blush in her cheeks. She held out her hand.

"Hello, Señor Palafox."

Antonio smiled down at her. His warm brown eyes looked directly into hers. "How do you do, Señorita." He took her hand, slowly raised it to his lips and brushed it softly. His eyes never strayed from hers.

A shiver ran through Sofia's body and she withdrew her hand quickly.

"Hello, Sofia," Isabela said coolly.

Sofia tore her eyes away from Antonio's playful gaze and looked at Isabela. She hoped desperately that her unusually high color could not be detected by Isabela's imperious eyes.

"Hello, Isabela," she said breathlessly. "You must be happy to have your brother home."

Isabela flashed a smile in Antonio's direction. But when she looked back at Sofia, her expression was hard. "Yes, but now we must go. Doña Ana is dying to meet Antonio."

Forcefully, Isabela pulled her brother away from Sofia and Estrella, and threaded her way through the groups of people still bartering with the traders. Sofia, watching the pair retreat, felt a strange and sudden loss. She was about to turn back to her father's wagon when she saw Antonio turn and look back. Their eyes locked for a brief moment, then he was gone.

WANDA DIONNE has written three historical novels for young adults. She says, "My heroine is always a young person with a problem. You might call her a victim. The important thing is that she does not remain a victim for long. I want my books to entertain first, and then to foster a love for our country's wonderful history. But if my readers gain insight about the strength that lies within themselves, I will be satisfied that I have done my job well." Ms. Dionne lives in The Woodlands, Texas, near Houston.

Historical Adventure and Romance with the AMERICAN DREAMS Series from Avon Flare

SARAH ON HER OWN
by Karen M. Coombs   78275-8/$3.99 US/$5.50 Can
When she leaves England to sail to the New World, love is the last thing Sarah expects to find.

PLAINSONG FOR CAITLIN
by Elizabeth M. Rees   78216-2/$3.99 US/$5.50 Can
Caitlin's heart belonged to the American West . . . and the man who taught her to love it.

INTO THE WIND
by Jean Ferris   78198-0/$3.99 US/$5.50 Can
Nowhere in her dreams did Rosie imagine sailing the high seas on a pirate ship!

SONG OF THE SEA
by Jean Ferris   78199-9/$3.99 US/$5.50 Can
Together Rosie and Raider challenge the dangers of uncharted waters and unfulfilled dreams.

WEATHER THE STORM
by Jean Ferris   78198-0/$3.99 US/$4.99 Can
Fate conspired to keep Rosie and Raider apart, yet their love was even more powerful.

For Heavenly Romance Turn to

TEEN ANGELS

by CHERIE BENNETT and JEFF GOTTESFELD

#1: HEAVEN CAN'T WAIT   78247-2/$3.99 US/$5.50 Can
Cisco has to earn her angel wings . . . by helping the world's
sexiest rock star.

#2: LOVE NEVER DIES   78248-0/$3.99 US/$5.50 Can
This is one test Nicole can't fail . . . if she intends to get her
wings.

#3: ANGEL KISSES   78249-9/$3.99 US/$5.50 Can
Melody's Earth assignment may win angel points . . . but will it
cost her her boyfriend?

#4: HEAVEN HELP US!   78577-3/$3.99 US/$5.50 Can
Cisco has a new earthly assignment—reform a horse killer.

#5: NIGHTMARE IN HEAVEN   78578-1/$3.99 US/$4.99 Can
There's a new girl in teen heaven, and she's after Melody's
boyfriend!